# The Edge of the Abyss

by

Michèle Phoenix

*For Chance and Riley*

© 2005 Michèle Phoenix
All Rights Reserved.

No part of this publication may be reproduced, stored in a retrieval system, or transmitted, in any form or by any means, electronic, mechanical, photocopying, recording, or otherwise, without the written permission of the author.

First published by Dog Ear Publishing
4010 W. 86th Street, Ste H
Indianapolis, IN 46268
www.dogearpublishing.net

ISBN: 1-59858-089-2
Library of Congress Control Number: 2005936917

This book is printed on acid-free paper.
This book is a work of Fiction. Places, events, and situations in this book are purely Fictional and any resemblance to actual persons, living or dead, is coincidental.

Printed in the United States of America

## Chapter One

The pier seemed endless.

It jutted out at a right angle from the shore and arced heavenward, falling out of sight where it merged with the horizon. On one end, it was anchored to the oil-stained pavement of a parking lot where cars rusted by salt air had been replaced for a few days by the swirling laughter of carnival rides. The rotund owner of a *barbe à papa* stand handed billows of cotton candy down toward hungry eyes and sticky hands. Nasal music blared from the circle of a safari-themed merry-go-round where eager passengers astride placid elephants and roaring tigers reached for the stuffed animal dangled tantalizingly just beyond their reach. It swooped and circled, rose and fell until one lucky hand plucked it out of the resonant air.

Casey set down her suitcases and scanned the scene with unfocused eyes. She rubbed the blood back into fingertips turned white by the weight of her luggage and inhaled a lungful of Brittany's sea-scented air. A winded mother yelled "*Viens ici!*" as she snatched a toddler from the edge of the parking lot where terra firma crumbled in a stony escarpment down to the water's edge. Casey watched as the woman roughly released the denim-clad boy and sermonized him on the virtues of sticking close to mom. Her voice was sharp, her syllables clipped and machine-gun fast. The French language seemed more suited to rebuke than to romance, Casey mused. And French women, from what she'd gathered in twenty-four hours of travel, were louder than they were soft and harsher than they were gentle. She observed the little boy standing blankly under his mother's displeasure. He seemed not in the least flustered by her angry gesticulating and impatient discourse. He blinked behind round, red-rimmed glasses, and then tottered off in the direction of a crêpe stand. His mother followed behind, still ranting, leaving Casey to wonder which of the two was really in control.

Casey's stomach growled, reminding her that it had been six hours since she had grabbed her last meal from a *boulangerie* between the train that had brought her to Rennes and the bus that had brought her to the water's edge in Roscoff. As wonderful as the *baguette* of fresh bread and Brie cheese had tasted, they hadn't made a lasting impression on her appetite. With the smell of crêpes, waffles, and warm macaroons wafting toward her, she felt a lightheaded craving that *nearly* distracted her from her journey. But a quick glance at the reddening sky brought her focus back to the pier stretching endlessly into the rough water beyond the shore. She'd been warned that it was nearly a kilometer long and that she'd be wise to hire one of the cart-pulling locals who offered to deliver her luggage to the ferry for a few euros, but she had made it this far without help, and her new-found independence demanded that she make this final leg of the journey unassisted.

Casey slipped her heavy beige canvas bag over her shoulder and bent down to lift her suitcases. *Lift with your legs*, her dad had always advised her. She smiled at her posthumous obedience and marveled that the words of a man who had died nearly a decade ago still determined how she lifted luggage, how she balanced her checkbook, and when she mowed her lawn. Mowed. Past tense. Her lawn—along with her house, her furniture, and her career—was on another continent, relegated to her past as surely as her plans and hopes had been. When she'd flown over the Chicago skyline with jet engines roaring in her ears and looked down at the sun glinting off the tinted glass of skyscrapers, it had finally sunk in. And when her plane had veered off over Lake Michigan, leaving Illinois behind, she had looked away into the blue horizon as a finality that sucked the breath from her lungs became reality.

This, then, was her future. The pier stretched over waves breaking on the rocky shore, curving up in the middle and sloping down toward the dock where Casey would board a ferry for her twenty-minute ride to the Ile de Batz. A late-day mist obscured the island and muffled the horn of the ferry making its way across the two-kilometer expanse of water to the Roscoff port. She squared her shoulders, released a breath she hadn't realized she'd been holding, and set off down the white-railed walkway with determination in her step. She would not turn back. From the moment she had decided to make this trip to France, she hadn't accepted retreat as an option—not when she'd reached her conclusion in the middle of a grief-stricken night, sitting at her sister's kitchen table in the Glen Ellyn suburb of Chicago, not when she'd announced her plans to her stunned family, not when she'd booked a one-way ticket to a country she'd never visited before, and not when she'd said her final goodbyes in the O'Hare terminal, painfully relinquishing the last human vestiges of a life she was leaving behind.

Darkness fell quickly in the Finistère area of France. By the time Casey reached the end of the pier, the lights lining it had come on. They made it look like a celestial walkway between raucous reality and misty oblivion. Even at this distance, Casey could hear the chaos of carnival mayhem and feel the bass pulses of amplified techno excess. Walking against the wind with her luggage had left her breathless and warm despite the dropping temperature. She paused for a moment to unbutton her brown corduroy jacket and catch her breath.

"We're heading to church," Layle called from the other side of the bathroom door. "You want to come along?"

Her shoulder-length auburn hair wrapped in a white towel, Casey sat at the vanity staring straight ahead as her face materialized out of the steam coating the mirror. Wide-set brown eyes, deep in their color and their awareness, gazed back at her. They were not the eyes of a survivor. They were the eyes of a victim still trapped, looking toward the light and believing it to be a hallucination. Dark circles accentuated their haunted expression and marred the pale, dull whiteness of her skin. Even the smattering of freckles that had once graced her dainty nose seemed to have faded with her vitality. She exerted superhuman willpower and tried to curve her lips into a smile. Her mouth had always been small. It looked smaller yet now that it had lost its ability to reflect anything other than stunned disbelief.

"Casey?" Layle called again before Casey's determination yielded the desired smile.

"I think I'll stay home," she said in a voice that barely made it through the bathroom door to her sister's ears.

"You sure?"

She heard the sadness in Layle's voice and wished she had the strength to do something to relieve it. But she hadn't had the energy to go out to dinner, walk to the park, or attend a church service in weeks. Just staring at herself in the bathroom mirror required more endurance than she possessed.

"I'm sure, Layle," she said in as strong a voice as she could muster. "Tell the kids I'll watch Nemo with them after lunch."

The silence on the other side of the door lasted a few seconds before Casey heard Layle's footsteps retreating. There were muffled instructions for the kids to hurry up, for Toby to comb his hair, for Melissa to brush her teeth. Troy, Layle's husband, announced that he'd be waiting in the car. Casey heard the garage door rumble open and the car's engine start. Moments later, the front door closed softly behind Layle and the kids.

Silence.

Casey loathed it and cherished it. It was her companion, her tormentor, her healer, and her challenger. It was empty—

hollow—yet so haunted that it felt crowded as it settled over her mind and forced the weary droop of her shoulders. She had moved from the oppressive stillness of her home to the guest room of Layle's suburban house to escape the silence. Yet even with several miles of distance between her past and her temporary present, the stillness weighed unforgivingly on her consciousness.

Casey's chilled fingers idly toyed with the gold necklace hanging in the V of her white terrycloth robe. Her hand was slim and shook with an almost imperceptible tremor. She had always based her perception of people in part on their hands. How their hands touched a child. How they held a steering wheel. How they moved to accentuate speech and how they lay when they were at rest. She wondered what others would assume about her if they could see her hands now. Once manicured and well groomed, her fingernails now were ragged and unkempt, her skin dry and sallow.

The symbolism didn't escape Casey's mind.

With a resigned sigh, she pulled the towel from her hair and reached for a comb. She would deal with the details of life later.

Right now, she needed to wrestle with the silence.

The ferry waited by the *embarcadère* at the end of pier. It was a small craft with only enough seating for two dozen people inside and a small area of standing space in the bow for overflow passengers. Just a handful of locals had arrived with the boat, and Casey was the only person boarding for its return trip to the island. The ferry's pilot, a terse middle-aged man whose leathery face wore the ravages of a lifetime on the water, jutted his chin toward her luggage. She wasn't sure if the gesture was an offer to help or a command to hurry up. She apparently hesitated too long, because he stepped onto the landing in one long, arthritic stride, nearly shoving her aside in the process, and stepped back onboard carrying her suitcases as if they weighed nothing. He dumped them unceremoniously on the floor of a shelved area behind the pilot's cabin, cast off the lines anchoring the ferry to the dock, then stepped inside and prepared to maneuver away from Roscoff.

Hearing the motor's roar snapped Casey into action. She held the strap of her bag tightly and stepped across the broadening space between the dock and the boat. She teetered a little as she made her way to the bow, then braced her hands on the railing as the deck shifted beneath her feet. The salty air whipped strands of auburn hair across her face and stung her eyes. She watched as the ferry picked up speed, following the colored buoys that lined the deeper canal at the center of the waterway. She caught faint glimpses of a rugged shoreline through the mist, of areas where the light shining through windows of dark houses seemed more concentrated, and of vaster expanses where neither light, nor vegetation, nor human construction seemed to interrupt the rough landscape.

The ferry's horn startled Casey. She let out an involuntary gasp, covering her throat with a cold hand. When she turned and squinted toward the pilot's cabin, wondering why he had sounded the blast, she found him staring straight ahead into the darkening night. There was no expression on his sea-worn face. His jaw was set, his eyes were narrowed, and though he must have seen her turn, he didn't glance her way.

Looking back toward the Ile de Batz, Casey drew her jacket close and crossed her arms across her chest to ward off the chill of the wind. With every second, dim lights became brighter and the structures of the island's harbor came into focus. She saw the cement contours of the jetty, the small crafts moored alongside it and the outcropping of rocks from which it seemed to grow. Beyond the jetty, the masts of yachts and fishing vessels in the harbor swayed lazily, their paint reflecting the beams from a small semaphore perched high above the harbor. Between the water and the semaphore, stone homes climbed the hill, expanding out from the church steeple at their center along streets running parallel to the shoreline. Streetlights outlined and highlighted their uneven facings, illuminating stone walls and rustic wooden shutters.

As the ferry neared the jetty, a young man who had been lounging on the outcropping of rocks stood up and waited for the boat to come alongside the striped fenders lining the cement edges of the *embarcadère*. When the boat was still a fair distance away, he leapt aboard, grabbed the stern line, and leapt off again, securing the line to one of the piles along the jetty. The captain turned off the engine and, without a glance at Casey, brushed past her to throw the stem line to the young man chatting in lilting syllables while he worked.

Casey tried not to react as he laughingly complimented the captain on his "catch". She bit her tongue when the captain replied that all the island needed was another *imbécile d'américaine*. She knew that American tourists weren't always welcome in France, but being called an imbecile still took her by surprise. The captain dropped the chain across the opening in the gangway where she had boarded the ferry.

*"Aide la, tu veux?"* he instructed his young helper with the first trace of a smile Casey had seen yet, *"Elle est pas fichu de descendre de la vedette sans tomber à l'eau."*

His final insult was too much for Casey to take in silence. Quelling her insecurities, she strode to the captain's side. With her bag clutched to her stomach, she tried to make eye-contact with his averted gaze as she spoke in French for the first time since her arrival in the country. Her voice was soft but firm.

"I am not an imbecile," she said in a well-practiced accent, "and I am capable of disembarking without falling in."

The captain glanced quickly in her direction without actually meeting her gaze, then turned away with a grunt and reached for her luggage. He tossed the suitcases to the young man on the pier with incredible ease and, with a "*Salut*" mumbled toward his helper, retreated to the cabin and his logs. Casey didn't waste her breath on him and instead cast a strained smile at the young man standing on the jetty with one of her suitcases in each hand.

"You want me to carry them?" he asked. He was a gangly young man with a full head of unruly red hair and a cheerful, innocent countenance that seemed a stark contrast to the captain's surliness. Casey was about to take him up on his offer, though reluctantly, when the captain bellowed at the boy to clean the deck. After a moment of hesitation, he set down the luggage and meekly stepped aboard, leaving Casey standing alone, jet-lagged to the point of nausea, emotionally worn out and aghast at the men who were leaving her helpless in a strange, dark place.

She knew there were no cars or taxis on the island and that the only motorized vehicles were tractors and municipal trucks. With few options and very little energy left, she seized on what shreds of determination she still felt and set off toward the village lining the port. A curved road skirted the water's edge then climbed toward the church above the harbor. Grateful for the wheels on her suitcases, Casey walked for several minutes pulling them behind her. She stopped at the foot of the hill and took the map she'd printed off the Internet from her bag. After a few deep breaths, she set off again, pulling her luggage uphill now, her lungs rebelling at the workout.

*Just a little bit farther*, she kept telling herself as she walked through narrow streets lined with stone houses. Aside from slivers of light escaping around closed shutters, there were few signs of life on the Ile de Batz. Seven p.m. on the island felt like midnight back home, and the noise of her suitcases dragging on the pavement seemed inordinately loud. The near-human sound of a cat mewing forlornly sent shivers down Casey's spine. She forced a faster pace, passing the church and its cemetery, veering off to the right, then uphill again. She was walking along a low stone wall that overlooked the port when a shadow stirred in the dark. She smothered a startled gasp but wasn't able to quell the impulse that drove her quickly across the street and into the relative safety of a streetlight's glow. She looked into the shadows and saw the red tip of a cigarette vaguely illuminating a man's face, but not brightly enough for her to distinguish anything more than a scruffy beard and hooded eyes.

Casey opened her mouth to speak, then realized she had nothing to say. Her suitcases were still on the other side of the street where she'd abandoned them, just a few feet away from the stranger whose smoke tinged the air with a hint of warmth.

He said nothing.

She said nothing.

The silence stretched and tautened.

When Casey's discomfort outgrew her intimidation, she took a step toward the stranger and, clearing her throat to dispel any tremor of fear from her voice, dared to speak.

"Is this the way to the Kermadec house?" she asked in French.

The glowing tip of his cigarette moved up and down once. She waited for an answer.

"Alright," she said when the silence had lengthened again. "I…" She was at a loss. "Thank you," she said under her breath—and wondered as soon as she had said it what she was thanking him for.

With a courage she didn't feel, she crossed the street to retrieve her luggage and, resisting the impulse to run rather than walk, resumed her uphill trek. A few seconds later, with the sound of her breathing in her ears and forty-eight hours without sleep weighing down her steps, she felt more than she heard a presence beside her. The smell of cigarette smoke identified her follower just before a male hand reached for the handle of one of her suitcases. She was turning to confront the stranger with a hollow threat when she realized he had moved to her other side and was relieving her of her second suitcase as well.

"Oh," she said dumbly as he stepped around her and set off in the direction of the address she was seeking. He was walking too slowly to be making an escape, so she assumed the best, which was a stretch under those circumstances, and followed meekly behind her mute benefactor. She didn't try to speak again, she didn't ask him where he was going, and she didn't question his motives. He led her to a split in the road where one branch headed into a steeper incline toward the semaphore and the other curved to follow a path parallel to the waterline far below. There was a wooden gate at the V in the road, hanging slightly askew on its hinges and overgrown with tall weeds climbing along the red brick that framed it. The stranger set down her suitcases next to the gate. He dropped his cigarette butt and ground it under the toe of a well-worn sneaker. Then, without a word, he walked away from Casey into the deepening darkness shrouding the small town.

Casey looked more closely at the gate in front of her and saw the street number she'd been looking for hanging loosely from a single nail on the crossbar.

For the first time since she'd said her goodbyes at O'Hare airport, she felt tears flooding her eyes.

She was home.

## Chapter Two

Casey wondered if the gate would fall off its hinges when she opened it. But she was fairly sure the weeds overwhelming it would hold it up even if it became disconnected from the brick posts on either side of it.

She cast a final glance at the silent stranger who had so unexpectedly led her to this place. Silhouetted against a single streetlight, he walked with slow, indolent steps, then disappeared around the corner. Wherever he was going, he was in no hurry to get there.

But there were more pressing concerns on Casey's mind than the stranger's destination. With an unsteady hand, she reached over the gate and slid the bolt on the other side. Pushing the gate open against the protestations of rusted hinges, she drew her luggage into the overgrown yard and left it there. In the darkness, it was hard to see the path that led to the front steps of the house. She felt its unevenness as she made her way over packed earth and loose stones, feeling tall weeds brushing against her legs. Six cement steps framed by wrought-iron railings led up to the door.

As she reached into her pocket and retrieved the key to the front door, a recent conversation echoed in her mind.

"It's three a.m., Louise."

"Over there, it is! It's already nine here. So tell me, luv. How are you holding up?"

Casey wasn't ready to let Louise off the hook, as disarming as her thick British accent was. "Louise," she said in a voice she usually reserved for her students, "Layle has kids and a husband who get up in three hours. Couldn't you have waited until morning to call?"

"You know me and math, Dearie. The time difference always messes with my brain."

Casey sighed. Louise had been part of the family lore for so long that it felt like she was a relative, yet they had only met face-to-face once. She was the daughter of a man who had fought with Casey's grandfather near the shores of Normandy. A high ranking member of the French *résistance*, Jacques Kermadec had ridden a moped for forty-eight hours straight during the Allied invasion, siphoning gas for his *Solex* out of stranded cars and tractors, and ferrying information about German troop movements and targets to the American front line. On the third day after the *débarquement,* a German sniper had picked him off as he rode through a small village toward the Allied troops who had set up camp in the local church. Seriously wounded and exposed to more enemy fire, he had resigned himself to die. But he hadn't counted on the loyalty of the troops he had aided. While Allied fire diverted the attention of the German soldiers, a solitary American Marine stole through the wooden doors of the church and made his way to his wounded comrade's side. He hoisted him onto his shoulders and carried him back to the church, earning a return ticket to Illinois when a bullet tore through his knee nearly severing his leg.

Several years after the end of the war, Jacques had tracked down Casey's Grandpa Joe to thank him for saving his life. The long-distance friendship that ensued had survived Jacques' passing and lived on in Louise's twice-yearly calls. When the phone rang on December 25th and June 8th, the exact anniversary of Jacques' rescue, the family knew to expect to hear Louise at the other end of the line. Jacques had moved his family to England when Louise was a small child, and her charming accent somewhat tempered her occasional lack of tact.

This was only the third time Louise had called on a day

other than her usual routine. The first time had been to share the news of her father's death. The second had been to announce that she was in Chicago and taking a cab to their home. And this time was to make Casey an offer she hadn't expected to hear.

When Layle had woken her and announced that Louise was on the phone, Casey had thrown on her robe and headed to the kitchen to use the phone that sat on the counter next to the unsightly clay vase Toby had made in kindergarten.

"It's so good to hear your voice, Casey," Louise now said, "even if it *is* the middle of the night over there. I've been concerned about you."

Casey massaged her temple with the tip of her index finger. "That's kind of you, Louise. But I'm doing alright. Really."

"Well, I had an epiphany a few minutes ago that I simply couldn't wait to share with you!"

"An epiphany?" Casey asked warily.

"*Une révélation divine!*" Louise declared dramatically, her voice loud enough to make Casey wonder if a telephone was really necessary to share her "divine revelation". When Casey didn't respond, Louise went on undeterred. "Layle emailed a few days ago and explained a bit about why you moved in with them, and I had an absolutely scrumptious idea. How would you like to take an extended vacation in Europe?"

"Louise, I'm not sure now is a good time for me to..."

"It's not so much a vacation as a change of scenery, I suppose," Louise interrupted. "It's just that my family home on the Ile de Batz has been sitting there for years now, completely uninhabited except for summers, and I think a bit of island life might be just what the doctor ordered for you."

Casey was suddenly wide-awake. "What are you saying, Louise?"

A warm chuckle made its way from England to Illinois. "I know this must be completely unexpected," Louise said with a smile in her voice, "but I thought it would be worth offering it to you if you'd like to use it. The house has been in the family forever. It's the farthest thing from a mansion, but the island is quiet and quaint. It'll be nothing but you and God's creation, luv, and I thought that might sound good to you right about now."

A thousand questions played bumper cars in Casey's mind. "Where did you say this island is?"

"Just off the coast of Brittany. Near Roscoff and the English Channel. The house is a bit rustic and the locals take some getting used to, but it's safe and it's clean. You can move in as soon as you wish and stay as long as you need. What do you think?"

Casey was incapable of speech. She felt the flutter of something optimistic in her chest and held the phone more tightly to her ear as the first hint of excitement she'd felt in months made her breathe a little faster.

"It's rent-free, of course," Louise continued, "so you can't beat the price... You still there, dear?"

"I... Yes! Yes, I'm right here, Louise..."

"Oh, good. These blasted international phone connections are so unreliable, aren't they?"

"Louise..."

"You don't have to give me answer now, luv. Think it over for a while and let me know what you decide, alright? The house isn't going anywhere."

But Casey didn't need any longer to mull it over. Though she had spent weeks in a fog, the immediate future was suddenly as clear and urgent as the forces that made her departure necessary.

"I'll start looking for a ticket tomorrow, Louise," she said. "Tell me what I need to know."

∞

And here she stood, just three weeks later, on the threshold of Jacques Kermadec's family home, marking the commencement of... But of what? Not for the first time, Casey wondered about the wisdom of her move and the rationale that had driven her to it. She had neither run *from* anything nor rushed *toward* something. She had simply left all that was familiar, crossed an ocean with two suitcases, and arrived in a foreign country where only the language held no mysteries. Ten years as a high school French teacher had prepared her well for the linguistic challenges ahead, but she felt completely unequipped when she contemplated life on an island that seemed as remote from the North American lifestyle as the pervading turmoil in her mind was from serenity.

Her key slid easily into the lock. She turned it, opened the door, and stepped inside.

Her first impression was of a stale, musty scent. The entryway smelled like an attic closed up during a damp summer day or the cushions on the well-worn, ancient sofa of her family's summer cottage. The air felt close and the darkness added to its oppression. Casey felt along the wall beside the door until her hand connected with a switch projecting at eye-level from the cool plaster. A single bulb hanging from the high ceiling by its wires lit the long hallway that led from the front door to a rickety staircase on the opposite end of the house. There was a coat tree just to the right of the door on which an olive-green windbreaker, a yellow umbrella, and a brown fisherman's hat hung. A pair of dirty grey rubber boots sat underneath it, flanked on one side by a large flashlight and on the other by what appeared to be a small metallic toolbox.

There were two doors that led off of the long hallway. Both were closed. Casey opened the one on the left and again felt along the wall for a light switch. Another bare bulb came to life, illuminating a kitchen's white walls and fake-tile linoleum. Casey walked through a strand of spider's web as she made her way to the kitchen sink. She wiped the sticky strand from her face and stopped between light grey, plastic-covered cupboards that didn't look quite straight and a low sink that appeared to be made of yellowed Plexiglas. The small window above the sink was streaked with grime, its frame covered in lime-green cracking paint. There was a small fridge next to the sink, only about three feet tall and in desperate need of scrubbing. Its unplugged cord lay draped over the door, propping it open. Casey located the nearest outlet and plugged the fridge into the wall. It hummed and rattled, seemed to deliberate for a moment, then settled into a congested-sounding drone.

The dining area was on the other end of the room, near a window that faced out toward the front yard. Casey guessed daylight would reveal a view of the harbor, but for now, the window framed nothing but darkness. A small Formica table and three matching chairs, in the same shade of grey as the cupboards, sat under yet another bare bulb. On the wall farthest from the door, a rustic and clearly ancient hutch held a mismatched assortment of teacups, mugs, glasses, and various knickknacks. Just to the left of the door was a waist-high bookcase on which an outdated tape deck sat.

With a deep sigh, Casey made a slow turn, taking in the mildew stains around the windows, the deep gouges in the beige and brown linoleum, the burdened cobwebs spanning the corners of the ceiling, and the shrunken blue sponge sitting in a muck-caked dish next to the dirty taps on the filthy sink. A long piece of tie-dyed fabric hung from ceiling to floor between the hutch and the cabinets. Casey assumed, by the way the orange and lime-green fabric swayed, that it might be covering a doorway. She pushed the makeshift curtain aside and found herself staring at a seatless toilet bowl. A quick perusal of the space around the doorway revealed no light switch, and a glance at the ceiling confirmed Casey's misgivings. With no door, no toilet seat and no light fixture, the tiny bathroom was obviously an afterthought. The 3- by 5-foot space seemed to have been tacked on to the original structure of the house without even the benefit of a door to cover the hole that had been punched through the wall and roughly cemented into a rectangular shape.

Casey instructed herself not to sigh again and exited the kitchen, deliberately leaving the light on behind her. Another door opened across the hall from the kitchen. She gingerly turned the knob, pushed the door open, located the light switch, and stepped into the living room. Completely surrounded by dark wood paneling, it was a cozy room with one window facing front and two others flanking a wide fireplace on the far wall. Casey tried to concentrate on the good points of the room, letting her gaze linger on the ornately carved mantle, the antique buffet and armoire on either side of the door, the hard-wood floor, and the broad, worn, sit-in-me leather armchair pulled up to the fireplace. What she ignored was more cobwebs, more dust, more filthy area rugs, another bare light bulb, and sofas that looked so old and so soiled that even the Salvation Army might reject them.

But this was no time for discouragement, so Casey left the living room, its lights still on, and headed to the staircase at the far end of the entrance hall. The steps creaked and groaned as she climbed to the second floor. A door at the top of the stairs, intended to keep the warmth of the fireplace from escaping into the sleeping quarters, squeaked dryly as she pushed it open. Casey found herself standing in a small hallway, no larger than a North American walk-in closet, from which two rooms extended. The one to her right was small, made smaller by the slanted ceiling that paralleled the shape of the roof above it. The other was much larger, with windows and skylights that made it feel less cramped. A large bed against the far wall under the highest portion of the ceiling seemed to Casey's exhausted mind like a piece of heaven on earth. And there were actual light fixtures in wood and brown glass on either side of the bed, which was a great improvement on the bare bulbs she had encountered until then.

Casey pulled back the orange and brown blanket on the bed and found what appeared to be clean sheets beneath it. A closer look revealed nothing suspicious—only the promise of several hours of uninterrupted sleep. Further exploration could wait until morning. What Casey needed now, aside from an hour or so in her sister's Jacuzzi, was rest. She moved tiredly down the stairs, through the hall, out the front door, and down the sloped path to the gate where she had left her luggage. Desperation lent her strength. She carried her suitcases up the path and into the living room and, leaving them open on the hardwood floor, went to the kitchen to brush her teeth. She locked the front door, turned off all but the entryway lights, and then, with her favorite pair of flannel pajamas in hand, climbed the stairs to her bedroom.

"*Allez-y, ma petite dame! Il est frais, il est beau, et il coûte pas trop!*"

The voice was shrill, loud even after it passed through the walls of the house, and most definitely French.

"*J'ai des pétoncles! J'ai du Saint Pierre! J'ai tout ce qu'il vous faut!*"

"I don't want any fish," Casey moaned as she pulled her pillow over her head. But the musty smell of the pillow and sudden realization of where she was brought her mind to instant alertness. A glance around the room confirmed that it hadn't all been a dream. She pushed back the blankets and stepped to the window that faced the front of the house, releasing the latch that held it shut, then swinging open the peeling dark-green shutters outside. And there it was: a breathtaking view of the harbor, the small rocky islands beyond it, and, in the distance, the town of Roscoff. Casey breathed in a lungful of crisp salt air and closed her eyes as she released it. *I'm really here,* she thought. But she wasn't sure if the relief of that realization was in where she was or where she *wasn't*. She supposed the next few days would tell, but in the meantime, she had some exploring to do.

Closing the window, she draped a blanket over her shoulders and went downstairs to rummage through her suitcases. She found comfortable black exercise pants and a soft purple v-neck sweater. Running her fingers through her tangled hair, she headed for the front door, unlocked it, and stepped outside.

The fish-lady had set up her table on two wooden horses right next to the gate at the bottom of the path leading to Casey's front door. There were three crates on the table, each containing an assortment of fresh fish. Casey could smell them from the front stoop of her house. She ignored the instinctive impulse to recoil from the odor and wandered down the path to the gate instead.

If the fish-lady saw her coming, she gave no sign of it.

*"Salut, Pierrot!"* she called to the young man passing by. It was the same young man who had met Casey's ferry the night before and he looked just as disheveled in the daylight as he had in the dark. He lifted a casual hand toward the fish-lady as he turned onto the path leading uphill toward the semaphore. He walked leaning forward, as if the pull of gravity propelled him onward.

Casey stood just inside her yard, a few feet from the large woman peddling the day's catch to locals and tourists. The yard was overgrown, as Casey had suspected it would be. All that grew were tall, ragged weeds and patches of nettles.

Casey cleared her throat and looked toward the robust middle-aged woman rearranging the fish in one of her crates. The woman glanced her way, her eyes narrowing in quick appraisal, then returned her attention to the fish.

Casey stood in silence a moment longer, unsure of how to proceed. When a young couple pushed rented bicycles past her stand, the lady broke into a smile and loudly made them her best offer, claiming they would find no better fish for that price anywhere. The young couple, impeccably dressed in stylish sports attire, asked the lady if they could reserve their order and pick it up when they were finished bicycling around the island.

The lady nearly bent over backwards in her willingness to grant their request. As cold as she had been with Casey, she seemed amazingly friendly with the well-groomed tourists who looked like they belonged anywhere but on the Ile de Batz.

As the lady wrapped their order in newspaper and placed it back on the ice lining the bottom of the crates, Casey looked more closely at the fish and wondered how anyone could eat it. From their wide-open eyes to the slimy shine of their scales, they were as unappetizing as the flour-and-water concoctions Melissa used to make for her, rolling the dough out on her bedroom floor and collecting numerous cat hairs in the process. Next to the fish were creatures Casey could only describe as giant red spiders. That they were *edible* was one thing, but that someone would actually *eat* them was another! Not for the first time, Casey wondered why a person who hated fish would strand herself on a fishing island. She only hoped there was a store nearby that sold *real* food.

When it became obvious that the fish-lady was not going to acknowledge Casey's presence, she took a deep breath and mustered some uncharacteristic boldness.

"Hi," she said in French, extending her hand over the wooden gate, "I'm Casey."

The lady turned her back on Casey and bent over to retrieve more fish from the bucket at her feet. Casey was stunned. She slowly lowered her outstretched hand and took a step backwards. The cold morning air blew through her sweater and, combined with the lady's frigid disposition, chilled Casey to the bone. She waited for the lady to straighten, waited while she arranged her fish, waited while she smiled and chatted with another group of tourists, and waited while she stood by her table in utter silence staring off at the open water beyond the harbor. For several minutes, Casey stood and waited to be acknowledged, but acknowledgment never came. Finally, defeated and shivering, she made her way back to the house and shut the door behind her.

Eager to wash away the weariness of travel and forget the failure of her first social contact on the island, Casey found a towel in one of her suitcases and headed... She was in the middle of the hallway when a horrifying thought gripped her. In her exploration of the house the night before, she had seen neither bathtub nor shower.

Casey felt a chill completely unrelated to the weather. She hurried through the kitchen to the tie-dyed fabric and, pulling it back, hoped last night's assessment of the size of the bathroom had been somehow skewed by jetlag. But it was just as small—and devoid of a shower—as she remembered it. She glanced at the stained sink and briefly contemplated washing her hair in it, but the thought was short-lived. Heading upstairs, she went straight to her large bedroom and found not even a washbasin there.

In a final, desperate hope, she crossed to the smaller of the two bedrooms and, stepping inside, prayed for a miracle. But the room was empty save for a bed and a small dresser. Casey was about to close the door when she noticed another door on the far side of the room. Cut out of the wood paneling that covered the walls, it wasn't noticeable at first sight.

Reaching for the small brass doorknob, she pushed the door open, stepped inside, and nearly wept in relief. There was no shower in the tiny bathroom, but the antique cast-iron tub with two small faucets and the diminutive triangular sink in the corner were the most welcome sight the island had offered so far.

"Auntie Casey, are you still in the bathroom?" Melissa called through the locked door. "Mom said we can watch Nemo while she makes lunch!"

Casey had no idea how long she'd been sitting at the vanity. The last thing she remembered was the family's departure for church. Had she really sat immobile for over an hour, staring at herself in the mirror?

"Casey?" It was Layle's voice now, tight with anxiety. "Are you okay? Open the door, Case."

As much as she understood her sister's concern, Casey was frustrated by it—just as she was frustrated by the sympathy of fellow-teachers, by the sincere words of long-time friends, by the gentle voice of her minister when he called and the sweet gestures of neighbors and acquaintances.

"She's not responding, Troy."

Casey decided she'd better open the door herself before her brother-in-law took a screwdriver to it. It took superhuman effort for her to get up off the padded stool and take two steps to open the door. As soon as the lock slid, Layle pushed into the room, concern and relief on her face.

"You've been in here this whole time?" she asked.

Casey pulled her robe tighter and went back to sit at the vanity. She arranged the cosmetics and perfume bottles in front of her until they were all in a line, their labels facing out. Then, with nothing left to focus on, she caught her sister's gaze in the mirror.

All her life, Layle had known what to say to make Casey feel better. She seemed at a loss for the first time in memory. Casey saw tears pooling in her sister's eyes and felt irrational anger. More sympathy, more pity, more understanding. She was drowning in kindness.

"I just lost track of time," she said a bit more gruffly than she had intended. When her sister shook her head in incredulity, Casey added, "And there's no reason for you to look at me like that."

"Like what?" Layle's tone was carefully controlled, but Casey could hear an uncustomary tremor in it. "Like I'm concerned because you've spent the last two hours sitting in a bathroom?"

"There's nothing wrong with…"

"You've been doing little more than sit and stare for weeks, Case."

"I'm sorry," Casey said without conviction.

"Don't be sorry." Layle sighed. "I just wish there was something I could do to…to…to *jumpstart* you somehow."

Casey laughed. Though it was the first time she had laughed since mid-August, it didn't put Layle's mind to rest—because the laugh was harsh, cynical, and devoid of any trace of humor. It was a laugh that belonged among the dead, not among the living.

"What can I *do*?" Layle begged.

The sisters stared at each other in the mirror and Layle felt, as she had for so long, that they were barely connecting. Where there once had been a powerful bond there now was a chasm. Casey's eyes were familiar but their emotion—or lack thereof—was completely foreign. Not for the first time, Layle wondered if the world had lost her sister too on that fateful August night.

Casey blinked, breaking the tenuous connection her sister's gaze had created. This was not a time for connection. This was not a time for love and concern. This was a time for… But for what? This was a time for *time*. Period. Time passing. Time anesthetizing. But not time healing. She wondered if the time for that would ever come.

Casey tossed her useless blow-dryer into one of her open suitcases and pulled her damp hair back into a ponytail. Why hadn't anyone told her that American appliances were useless in this country? She resigned herself to letting her hair air-dry during her time on the island. The last hour had been incredibly frustrating. She missed showers. Bathing in the tub had been more of a challenge than it ought to be. With one tap for cold water and a separate one for hot water, she realized when she tried to wash her hair that she would either freeze her scalp or scald it. She'd had to run downstairs for a pitcher in which to mix the hot and cold water, then she'd used it as an improvised shower. The bathroom was dirty, cramped and unheated. It had clearly been as much of an afterthought as the downstairs toilet, and Casey suspected that the guest bedroom and the claustrophobic bathroom had once been a single space.

As she headed downstairs, Casey contemplated her chances of finding a blow-dryer for sale on the Ile de Batz. Louise had warned her that she could buy basic groceries in a small store on the other side of the semaphore, but little else. Any larger shopping sprees would require a ferry ride to Roscoff and possibly a bus ride to the city of Morlaix, an hour from the shore. As Casey didn't want to venture off the island yet, she found her wallet, checked to make sure enough of the money she'd changed yesterday remained, and left her house to find the island's store.

The fish-lady continued her boisterous advertising as Casey stepped around her and headed up the hill toward the semaphore perched on the highest point of the island. The semaphore was a large, square construction from which a jumble of antennas and satellite dishes projected. It functioned much as a lighthouse would and served to communicate with ships through light signals and radio waves. The road that led past it was steep and narrow, and several tourists on bicycles barely avoided hitting Casey as they rounded the corner at the top and began their descent.

When she reached the top of the hill, Casey paused and looked around. The harbor lay behind her, bathed in the crisp clarity of a cool autumn sun. Casey could see the lush greenness of vegetation in yards and on the hills surrounding *Porz Kernac*. But on the other side of the semaphore, behind a row of mismatched houses, inhospitable, barren land led out toward the open water. The vegetation on the north half of the island was completely different from the vegetation in the south. Trees, bushes and lush fields stretched along the waterfront parallel to

Roscoff's cliffs. But just a kilometer farther, where the wind blew fiercely and carved deep trenches into the mobile sand, there were few homes, few trees, and only rocky formations interrupted the expanse of flat, dry land.

Casey could see horses and riders in the distance. She heard the muted sound of a tractor's diesel engine and the rhythmic cling of cables slapping against the masts of ships in the harbor. A dog barked, a seagull cried. She marveled that these were the only sounds reaching her ears. Even in the relatively quiet suburb of Glen Ellyn, there had always been the sound of traffic, the clanging of alarms at the railway crossing near her home, and the blast of a car stereo playing too loudly.

Five minutes later, Casey reached a small storefront covered in ads for lodging, tourist information and a large handwritten chart of the week's discounted items. There were only four short rows of shelves inside the store and the selection of groceries and household products was limited indeed. From the moment she walked in, Casey felt an uncomfortable silence. Conversations stopped and the attention of other shoppers seemed focused unusually intently on the products they were looking at. She caught a couple of covert glances between the cashier and the woman in a blue apron stocking shelves on the farthest aisle of the store. Only a couple of middle-aged British ladies talking at the back of the store broke the silence.

Casey feigned confidence as she picked up a red plastic basket and wandered down the aisles, smiling as she said soft hellos to averted eyes and closed expressions. Was it really possible that all these islanders already knew who she was and disliked her on sight? And what was it she had done to earn such antipathy? Louise had warned her that it might take some time for the locals to warm up to her, but this coldness was surpassing even her worst expectations.

When she'd found enough basics to get her through the next few days and chosen a postcard to send to Layle and the kids, Casey approached the single checkout line at the front of the store. The cashier dutifully typed each price into her antiquated cash register, neither looking at her customer nor returning her greeting.

"Can you tell me where the bakery is?" Casey asked as she was handing over a ten-euro bill.

The cashier looked toward the woman stocking the shelves as if requesting permission to speak. The woman shrugged her consent.

*"Rue du Phare,"* the cashier finally mumbled, handing Casey her change and turning her attention to the next customer in line. Casey thanked the cashier, pocketed the coins, and left the store.

## *Chapter Three*

Casey threw a pebble into the water and watched the ripples expand. She'd been sitting at the harbor's edge for several minutes watching the fishermen tending to their nets. A flock of noisy *goélands* swooped down to pluck from the water what the fishermen threw overboard. She had always been fascinated by flight, and observing seagulls had been one of her favorite activities since childhood. Now, perched on top of one of the smooth rocks lining the harbor, she felt the autumn sun warming her back and allowed her mind to wander to places she hadn't visited in months.

Ben. She could see his face as if he were standing in front of her at that moment: hazel eyes where confidence and need dueled constantly, thick blond hair, a little long, always swept back from his face, and warm, tan skin. His looks weren't striking, but something in his countenance set him apart from other students. His grades were nearly perfect, though his classroom interaction made Casey wonder if he was ever really there. He came alive only on the soccer field. In his element, he was a powerful player—single-minded in his pursuits and ruthless in his attacks. No one would have suspected the depths of thought and emotion he hid under such managed visibility.

∞

"Miss Jensen?"

Casey had been pushing through the school's front door when she heard the voice beside her. She turned and found one of her senior boys lounging against his backpack on the top step of the staircase leading to the high school's entrance. Ben hadn't so much as opened his mouth during a year of French classes, so Casey was rather taken aback by the sound of his voice. He pushed himself up and held out the worn black notebook he'd been writing in.

"What's this?" she asked, taking the notebook from him.

Ben looked down and stuffed his hands deep into his pockets, shrugging as he said, "Just some stuff I've been working on."

Roughly carved into the hard cover of the notebook were three words: *Book of Confusion*. Casey was hesitant to open it. If this was a journal, it surely contained personal information this young man wouldn't want a teacher to read.

Casey watched him shuffling his feet and wondered where to go from here. "Do you want me to read it?" she asked.

Ben glanced up for a moment, his eyes briefly making contact with hers then sliding back to the book she held in her hands. He pointed with an unsure finger to the ragged edges of the pages on which he'd written.

"Page sixty-four," he said, his voice sounding like it was on the verge of a pubescent crack. "You can read that one."

This was certainly a novel experience for Casey. Students usually ran like the plague from staff members, particularly when they encountered them outside the classroom. This young man not only wasn't running, but he was asking her to read something he had written. Casey assumed it wasn't a French assignment and wondered what had pushed the young man to present his writing to her.

"Page sixty-four?" She turned the pages, taking in the small, precise black writing on each of them, the sketches in the margins, and the neatly printed Roman numerals on the outside lower corner of each page. The entries were all dated, confirming Casey's assumption that this was indeed a journal. Some were written in prose and others seemed to break down into poetic stanzas.

When she got to page sixty-four, Casey scanned the first sentence, then looked quizzically at the student standing awkwardly in front of her.

"This isn't a French assignment," she said, stating the obvious.

He shrugged.

"Uhm…" Her brows drew together in thought as she tried to phrase her next question carefully. "Why exactly do you want me to read this?"

Ben looked toward a handful of teenage girls making their way into the school. He turned slightly from Casey, clearly trying to distance himself from being associated with a teacher. Not wanting to make him any more awkward than he was, Casey turned her attention to her book bag, rearranging books and papers that didn't really need it.

Once the girls had entered the school, Ben turned back toward Casey.

"I just thought you might like to read it," he said, and Casey thought she heard a hint of defiance in his voice.

"Well, I'd love to read it, Ben, and…well…I'm honored you'd want me to. It's just a little unexpected!" She smiled at him in what she hoped was a soothing way. She was way out of her depths. Ten years of teaching had prepared her to cope easily with planning lessons, grading assignments, and dealing with overachievers, underachievers, kleptomaniacs, liars, perfectionists and slackers. In the context of her classroom, she was capable of confronting pretty much anything her students threw at her. But this apparently random connection with a student who had, until that day, been little more than a seat-warmer in her classes left her feeling unprepared and out of sorts. She'd heard the horror stories about students stalking teachers and knew that outside-the-classroom contact should be the exception, not the norm. But she also realized that she was standing in a very public place with this young man who, for reasons only he understood, had chosen to share a bit of himself with her. There was no danger in reading a page out of his journal.

Casey opened the black notebook again, sat down on the top step, and began to read.

*April 14, 2004*

*Another Sunday. Another sermon. Another load of crap. How can intelligent people believe in god? It's such an obvious scam. There's nothing to worship in a god whose only goal seems to be torturing humanity into submission. His cruelty doesn't bother me as much as the idiot believers who promote his cause. There is NOTHING in this world that points toward god being in control. An intelligent person would see the evidence for what it is. Unfortunately, humans are flawed—as all of god's "perfect" creation is. Which leaves us wallowing in a cesspool of corruption, greed, immorality, hypocrisy and f\*\*\*\*\*-up faith.*

Casey slowly closed the book, her finger tracing the outline of the words carved into its cover. Ben didn't have a reputation for depth of thought or spiritual insight. He was adulated by the girls in his class and envied by many of the school's athletes. His soccer skills were above average and his charisma was undeniable, so much so that half the signs held up in the bleachers during soccer games referred to him more than to the team. He usually sauntered around the school with a strut and a closed expression, which made him all the more appealing to teenage girls in search of a challenge.

"Sit down, Ben," she said, patting the spot next to her on the step. "Tell me why you wanted me to read this."

Ben didn't sit. He moved to the other side of the flight of

stairs and propped himself against the wall, the epitome of the high school heartthrob, equal parts James Dean and Tom Sawyer. Casey respected his need for distance and talked to him across the five-foot space.

"Is this because of the topic we discussed last class?"

He shrugged, and this time it looked like agreement.

"About *The Little Prince*?"

His eyes met hers. The class had dealt with the Antoine de Saint-Exupéry classic about a young Prince stranded on earth after a fall from his star. In the course of conversation, the class had discussed humanity's basic need to believe that *something* existed beyond our planet, allowing Casey to articulate her belief in a benevolent, all-knowing God.

The topic had come at the end of the period and been so casual that she hadn't expected a response from anyone—and certainly not from Ben. Having read Ben's journal entry, however, she assumed it was written in reaction to that discussion and, more specifically, to her personal statements.

Casey waited for another group of students to go by before looking at Ben again and, with a sigh, saying, "So you want me to know that you don't believe in God."

Ben's voice was low, frustrated, and intense. "I don't have an opinion either way," he said, glancing up for a moment, then looking back at his shoes. "I just don't understand how anybody can believe he's this great thing when the world is as screwed up as it is. If there was a good god out there, he'd do something about it."

"And you think I'm an idiot for believing there is?"

He shrugged again.

Casey rose and took a couple steps to where Ben was standing. Handing the book back to him, she bent down a bit to catch his gaze and hold it. "You want to know what I think?" she asked quietly. "I think God does exist. I think He is good and kind and incredibly concerned about what *we're* doing to 'screw up' this world."

Ben let out a humorless laugh, dismissing her statement.

"And I don't claim to understand everything, but that's okay," Casey continued, choosing her words carefully. "We're not going to figure it all out—not from this perspective. It's just a question of trusting what we believe until we *know* for sure."

Ben stood against the wall for what seemed an eternity, immobile and silent, his book at his side. Casey hadn't ever seen him look so young.

"Well…thanks for sharing your writing, Ben," she finally said. "I'm glad you trusted me with it."

He shrugged.

"You're an excellent writer. Maybe you could do something with it—like getting something published in the school paper, for starters."

When Ben idly kicked at a stone in response, Casey figured his daily quota for verbal communication had been exceeded. She scanned the parking lot.

"Are you waiting for a ride?"

"No."

"Did you miss your bus?"

"No."

Casey realized he'd been waiting on the steps to intercept her as she left the building.

"Okay," she said breezily, "I'll see you tomorrow. Don't forget to memorize your vocab words."

She was turning to walk down the steps when his voice halted her.

"Miss Jensen?"

"Yes, Ben?"

He held his journal in front of him. "You can take it home and read the rest if you want to."

Casey wasn't sure how to react. That he would offer to let her read his writing was an honor, especially considering how invulnerable he usually was. But accepting his journal seemed too personal, too intimate, for a teacher/student relationship.

"I don't know, Ben... I'd feel bad taking your journal home with me. Maybe if you copy down a couple of your favorite entries and give them to me tomorrow?"

Ben opened his book and quickly turned pages. Arriving at the ones he was looking for, he ripped them from the binding and handed them to Casey.

"This one isn't bad," he said, turning to retrieve his backpack. "You can give it back to me whenever," he added as he walked down the stairs toward the bike rack by the curb.

Casey held the torn sheets in her hand and watched him go.

"Uh... Thank you! I guess..." But Ben was long gone.

With a shake of her head and an ironic smile, she folded the journal entry, shoved it into her bag alongside the folder of papers she had to grade before morning, and made her way to her car.

Casey observed a small fishing vessel named *Belle des mers* making its way into the harbor. It moved gracefully, effortlessly weaving between other boats until it came to its habitual mooring point where a dinghy waited, as it had all day, to take the boat's captain back to dry land. Shielding her eyes against the sun, Casey watched as the captain released the anchor. He went about his business in a calm, unhurried way, as if every action was a natural extension of who he was. Despite the distance that made all but his shape invisible to Casey, she thought he looked familiar. Something about the way he walked, the way he carried the day's catch. When he stopped and cupped his hands near his face, Casey finally made the connection. She couldn't be sure from this distance, but this fisherman lighting his cigarette bore a marked resemblance to the Good Samaritan who had carried her luggage to the Kermadec house when she'd arrived.

By the looks of the crates he lowered into the dingy, the day hadn't produced much profit. Louise had told her that the island was economically—and in every other way—depressed. Fishermen could no longer make a living from their trade. Commercial companies and new fishing regulations had made competition all but impossible. So, as averse as the islanders were to foreigners, they knew their survival depended on the day-tourists who made the ferry ride to the Ile de Batz for an afternoon of sightseeing—either on foot, on horseback, or on rented bicycles. But with the bitter cold of winter fast approaching, even *they* would become scarce.

Casey watched as the captain left his boat and climbed down to the dingy below. The hum of the small outboard motor reached her across the unruffled water. He came along the jetty, cut the motor, and tied off. Then, with two crates under one arm and one under the other, he began his long walk around the harbor. When he neared the end of the jetty, a stone's throw from where Casey sat, another familiar figure stepped into view.

"*Salut, Luke!*" Pierrot exclaimed, raising his hand in greeting and trotting over to relieve Casey's Samaritan of one of his crates. Casey listened more closely. "*Alors, la pêche a été bonne?*" the boy inquired in a loud, enthusiastic voice. Casey could have answered the question herself. If it only took two people to carry the crates, the fishing had *not* been good.

"*Pas trop mauvaise,*" Casey heard the stranger—Luke—say. She knew it was a statement based on low expectations. If he deemed the day's catch to be 'not too bad', it's that he hadn't expected much more than nothing.

Pierrot chatted on with his puppy-like enthusiasm, asking a thousand questions Luke never bothered to answer. Casey didn't look up as they passed behind her. Irrational embarrassment about her nocturnal suitcase-laden hike and her unexpected rescue kept her eyes on the harbor but her ears on Pierrot. She didn't know what Luke thought of the stranded tourist he'd assisted, nor did she want to know. Her short stay on the island had already taught her to keep her expectations in check. If she expected no kindness, she had a very slim chance of being pleasantly surprised.

The afternoon had passed quickly. Casey had gone to the bakery to buy a *baguette* for her now traditional bread-and-Brie lunch. The bread had tasted a bit stale to her, but she knew that all French breads were not the same and simply assumed the island *baguette* had a different recipe than what she'd had before. And then she got to work. A quick assessment of the Kermadec house revealed that there was enough to be done in the kitchen and the downstairs bathroom alone to keep her busy until the weekend. Fighting jetlag's gravity, she began with the sink, using the bleach and the scrubber she had bought that morning to turn it several shades brighter. While her gloves were on and the bleach was in her hand, she moved to the bathroom, taking down the musty sheet that separated it from the kitchen, and giving the toilet bowl, floor, and walls the kind of scrubbing that exhausted her, but left the bathroom smelling and looking much better. She threw out the sponge and gloves, then set to work in the rest of the kitchen.

Though Louise had told her to make herself at home, doing so would have required that she gut the kitchen completely and start over. She settled for emptying all the cupboards, washing them down, and organizing their contents in a much more logical manner. When the insides of the cupboards were clean, she tackled the windows, the walls, and the exterior of the room's furniture, using bleach on nearly everything and discovering that even ancient linoleum could liven up with the proper care. She found a plain white sheet upstairs that she hung in place of its tie-dyed predecessor.

With the kitchen cleaner and brighter than it had been the day before, Casey stood in the doorway and contemplated her achievement. Far from feeling relieved or more at home, however, she felt like an intruder in someone else's space. All her life, she had turned to cleaning as a therapeutic activity—when her personal life was complicated, when students were in trouble, when she felt lonely or underappreciated. And until recently, cleaning had felt like digging out from under whatever life threw at her. Today, it felt like digging a deeper hole to drown in.

A familiar constriction held Casey's lungs in a vise. She went to the living room and sat in the leather chair for a few minutes, taking deep breaths and straining to be calm. When her anxiety persisted, she opted for some fresh air. It struck her, as she stepped outside, that she had only seen a small part of the island. Though it wasn't large and biking around it would only require a couple of hours, she knew exploring it thoroughly would demand more energy than she currently possessed. So, pulling on a grey fleece jacket over jeans and a red turtleneck, she settled for heading to the only place she knew: the harbor.

And there she sat, perched high on a rock as the afternoon sun sank slowly toward the horizon. She shifted her position to follow Luke and Pierrot's progress. They completely circled the harbor before entering a small, grey stone building with a turquoise door and matching shutters. From a distance, Casey could see a large frame hanging next to the door. Above the door, a horizontal sign read, "*Le Bigorneau*", and a smaller sign below that stated, "*Bar-Restaurant*". Casey assumed the frame held a menu and that the covered *terrace* next to the building held tables and chairs during the warmer summer months.

Hunger pangs and the reddening sky reminded Casey of the time of day. She rose to go home, then realized she had nothing to go home *to*. The only reading she had brought with her was still too painful for her to open, and, aside from the tape deck in the kitchen, there was no form of entertainment in the Kermadec home. She did have a postcard to write, but the thought of formulating something meaningful, even if it was to Layle, was daunting. Casey briefly considered stopping in at the restaurant for a cup of coffee and a newspaper, but she wasn't sure about sharing space with the man she now knew as Luke.

He had been far from verbal on their first meeting, which left her wondering if his assistance had been motivated by pity, annoyance, or a helpful spirit.

∞

"Do you really think this will help you?" Layle's voice seemed strained, her eyes just a little fearful.

"I don't know," Casey answered, her own voice less than steady. "But it's worth a try, don't you think?"

Layle paced behind the couch where Casey sat. It was the day after Louise's call, and the courage Casey had felt in the middle of the night had begun to wane in the daylight.

Layle came around the couch and sat next to her sister. "Casey," she said, every ounce of her fear and concern in that single word.

"It'll do me good to get away. Change the scenery a bit."

"Just like moving in here with us did you good? You changed the scenery, Case, but the rest is still the same."

She was right. If anything, Casey's lethargy had deepened. When Layle had suggested that she move in with them, her arguments had been that life with the small family would provide diversion, activity and a caring environment. But the truth was that her sister had been scared of what might happen to Casey if she'd continued to live alone. Her family had witnessed the deterioration of her state of mind, and they worried about more than just her emotional well-being—they worried for her life.

"I think I need to do this," Casey now said.

"Who will be there for you if it's too hard?"

"Maybe that's exactly why I need to go. To prove to myself that I can stand alone." She saw the sadness in her sister's eyes and grabbed her hand. "Don't do that, Layle. Don't think that you should be able to *fix* me. Whatever this is isn't going away."

"And running scared will help?"

"Everything else I've tried hasn't."

"Tried? Everything you've *tried*, Casey? When was the last time you *tried* anything?"

"Layle…" Casey could feel herself withdrawing again, as she did every time anyone tried to reason with her, comfort her, or motivate her.

"When was the last time you tried stepping out the door? Putting on makeup? Ironing your clothes? Having more than a three-sentence conversation with Toby and Melissa?"

"I'm not doing this on purpose, Layle!" Casey retorted, her failure to conquer her demons driving her once again to anger. "I just don't know *how* to fix it!"

"So you've decided to fly half-way around the world?"

Casey took a calming breath and strove to organize her thoughts. "I know you've tried to help me, and Layle, I'm so grateful for all you and Troy have done for me."

"Case…" Layle began, but Casey held up her hand to halt her.

"I'm doing this, Layle. I'm going to France."

"But you've never even…!"

"I'm *doing* this."

This determination was a foreign feeling to Casey. She laid a hand on her sister's knee to soften her statement but didn't meet her gaze. Standing, she slowly made her way from the room, feeling as though she were treading into quicksand and hoping salvation would come after the worst was over.

Casey had always considered herself a night owl, but this was ridiculous. It was three a.m. on the Ile de Batz, but her body was still on Illinois time, and eight p.m. was just too early for sleep. So there she lay in her stuffy-smelling bed making a mental to-do list of things to buy and jobs to accomplish. Finding a laundromat in which to wash her bed linens was at the top of the list, followed by cleaning the rest of the house, writing Layle and the kids, and finding a miracle cure for the islanders' antipathy toward her.

Casey hadn't ever been the subject of such overt dislike. Her earliest memories were of an idyllic life made of gingham family picnics, flannel slumber parties, and starched Sunday services. All the staples of familial bliss were there: the white picket fence, the faithful golden retriever, the summer cottage by the lake, and the overstocked Christmas tree. She had grown up without ever a doubt of being loved. From the father-daughter dances in Junior High to the homemade cake her mom decorated for each of the girls' birthdays, she and Layle had been the center of attention and the focus of their parents' surplus of love. She felt sorry for children who grew up in more fragile families, where the ebbs and flows of life shifted the emotional balance of adults who lived too close to the edge. Casual observers might have called the Jensen family boring. To Casey, it had been a luxurious island of peace, harmony and affection in which to rest.

High school had yielded to college. Though her mind and body had evolved, her anchors had remained unchanged: God, family, hope, and love for others. They were the cornerstones of the life she loved so much. Though she had suffered heartbreak, struggled in classes, and seen some plans derail, she had never lost her unflagging belief in the important things. Until recently. And in the middle of the night on a small island off the coast of France, with her parents both gone and her sister an ocean away, God and family seemed as remote as the stars she could see through the skylight above her bed. Not that she wanted anything to do with God anyway. If He wasn't a hoax, He was at best a liar. As for hope and love, she didn't want to consider them at all. Though she had always thought they were salutary, she wondered now if they were really impotent—as hollow and powerless as her own existence.

"Miss Jensen?"

Ben again. Same time. Same place. Same blue backpack.

"Ben!" She reached into her book bag for the excerpt from his journal. "I meant to give these back to you, but I didn't want to embarrass you during class."

He took the papers she held out to him. Then he stood there. He shifted his weight from one foot to the other. He scratched the back of his head. He glanced at her, then glanced away. She marveled again at how different he was when his writing was involved.

"Tell me about the man on the beach," Casey prompted.

He met her gaze. "The guy in my story?"

Casey nodded. "The man waiting for the tsunami." Ben looked uncomfortable. "Why is he waiting?" Casey asked.

"I explained it in the story," he answered, impatience creeping into his voice.

"I know," she said, sensing that a head-on approach would be more productive, "and it's a brilliant metaphor for man's search for God. I'm just wondering why a guy who doesn't believe in tsunamis and is out to prove they don't exist would stand on the beach and wait his whole life for one to appear."

Ben's eyebrows drew together in thought. "If he waits his whole life," he finally said, "and never sees one, he'll be sure they don't exist."

"Or he'll be sure he was standing on the wrong beach," she said. Ben shrugged. "And doesn't waiting for something imply believing it *might* exist?"

Ben bent to retrieve his backpack and shoved the papers inside.

"How long have you lived in Glen Ellyn, Ben?" Casey asked in an attempt to direct their conversation to less delicate topics.

He straightened and pulled his backpack onto his shoulder. "A year and a half."

"And do you like it here?"

"I don't know."

"Well, no two schools are alike. It might take a little while to adjust."

Ben shuffled his feet and stared at an empty Coke can lying on the ground. "I was home-schooled before we moved here."

Casey was surprised. "Until your junior year in high school?"

He nodded.

"Well, your mom did a great job. Your grades are certainly above average." She sensed his discomfort and tried again to change the topic. "So where did you live before you moved here?"

Far from relieving the tension, her question seemed to increase it. He adjusted his backpack and started to back toward the stairs. Casey didn't want to let him retreat. "I'd love to read more of your writing, Ben," she said, hoping to halt his escape. "Why don't you try a more direct approach? Come up with three or four basic statements that say what's foremost on your mind," she suggested, not wanting to pressure him in any way but eager to understand the forces that motivated him. Ben turned his back with no acknowledgement of Casey's words and sauntered down the steps, reckless confidence back in his strides despite what she'd just witnessed. On an impulse, she turned and reentered the school, heading straight to the front office and greeting the secretary warmly.

"Still here, Casey?"

Casey smiled sheepishly. "I do need to get a life, don't I?"

The secretary reached into her top drawer and pulled out a quarter, which she handed to Casey. "Here's a quarter," she said. "Go out and *buy* one."

"You're an evil, *evil* person, Marilyn," Casey said with a

laugh, refusing to accept the quarter she had instinctively reached for.

Marilyn laughed and dropped the quarter back into the drawer. "What can I do for you, gorgeous?"

"Can I see the file on Ben Landon?"

The secretary rolled backward in her chair and quickly found Ben's file in one of the three large cabinets lining the far wall of the office.

"Benjamin James Landon," she read, pulling the file from the cabinet and handing it over to Casey.

"Thanks, Marilyn."

"You want to use Anna's chair? She's gone for the day."

Casey took her up on her offer and went to sit in the administrative assistant's chair at the desk across the office from Marilyn's. She opened Ben's file and leafed through the documents inside, finding his application form and pulling it from the stack. There were the standard answers to standard questions: date of birth, place of birth, social security number, educational history… It was under that last heading that Casey found the information she was looking for. Tajikistan. She made a mental note to pull out her atlas and wondered why Ben had been so hesitant to reveal where he'd lived before moving to Glen Ellyn.

"Marilyn," she called across the office, "you know where Tajikistan is?"

Marilyn shook her head without looking up from her typing. "It's over there with all the other *stans* isn't it? Pakistan, Uzbekistan, Afghanistan…"

"The other stans, huh?"

"Hey, if you don't like the answer, don't ask the question!"

Casey laughed and crossed the office, returning Ben's folder to Marilyn. "Actually, that's already a lot more than I knew. You're a genius, Marilyn. It's time for us to get you out of this office and into the classroom."

"That's what I've been telling the principal for years," Marilyn said with a flutter of her eyelashes.

Casey patted her friend's shoulder and headed back out to the parking lot with Ben on her mind. There was something about the young man that fascinated her. He was a walking contradiction, externally the all-American rebel with solid chances of attending college on a sports scholarship, and internally a foreign-raised intense philosopher whose sensitivity and lack of confidence seemed to cripple him. She didn't know whether to envy him or pity him. She did know that he had decided to reveal some of his thinking to her, for reasons only he knew, and that it was her responsibility to be worthy of his vulnerability.

## Chapter Four

When the church bells rang four times, Casey decided to suspend her disbelief in Louise's miracle cures and crawled out of bed to give her advice a try.

"Now, you're going to have to deal with jetlag, luv," Louise had warned during their last conversation before Casey's departure.

"My body will adjust in time."

"Your body might, but your mind won't! Take my word for it—you'll find yourself staring at the ceiling in the middle of the night with every inane detail of your life turning cartwheels under your skull."

"You're such a bearer of good news, Louise."

Casey's sarcasm didn't halt Louise's train of thought. "So here's my advice. If you simply cannot sleep, run yourself a hot footbath, then lie on the floor with your feet soaking and a warm, damp cloth on your forehead. It's imperative that you do this near your bed so you don't have too far to go once you start feeling the effects."

"Uhm… Okay." Casey looked around for a witness to this conversation, but Layle and the kids had gone to the video store.

"And don't try laying on a blanket or anything," Louise continued undaunted. "The whole purpose is for your body to be a bit uncomfortable while your two extremities get warm and fuzzy."

"Right."

"After about twenty minutes of this, remove the cloth from your forehead, dry your feet and crawl into bed. No quick movements though. You don't want to wake up what you've just put to sleep. I assure you that you won't last two minutes once you're back in the sack."

There was a lengthy pause while Casey mustered up a mental image of Louise's prescription. "You're kidding, right?" she finally asked.

"Dearie, I never joke about important things. If it's about chocolate, sex, or sleep, you can assume I'm being serious."

Louise's unbounded enthusiasm had *nearly* been enough to raise Casey's spirits. She had thought her imminent departure might have already helped ease the vise on her mind and heart, but it really hadn't altered anything. She'd felt empty when she was sedentary and without goals. Now she was just an empty person with a destination in mind. Nothing else had changed. Perhaps the distance would be a better remedy.

When the sun finally woke her and Casey slipped her feet to the floor, she found a pot of cool water sitting there. The damp face cloth next to it attested that her middle-of-the-night escapades hadn't been part of a convoluted dream. She remembered going downstairs to find the largest pot in the kitchen. She remembered filling it with warm water—she would have used *hot* water if the house's furnace were capable of producing any. She remembered carrying the pot and the rag upstairs, and she remembered directing an unpleasant monologue at the ceiling of her bedroom while she lay on the hard wood floor with her feet immersed in water and the warm cloth on her forehead. After several minutes of the prescribed inactivity, she said a few choice words to Louise, wherever she was, and crawled between the still-warm sheets of her bed.

That was the last thing she remembered. Either Louise was a genius or Casey was as manipulatable as the women she scorned who spent entire salaries on unproven miracle products. Whatever the case was, she had slept—and slept soundly—for five hours. It hadn't been a lengthy night, but it had been restorative nonetheless.

The shrill voice piercing through two layers of shutters and windows informed her that the fish-lady was back. Casey wondered why the woman had set up her table at that particular spot. Although it was at a crossroad of sorts, there were plenty of other intersections on the island. The voice bellowing at passers-by kept Casey sitting on the edge of her bed for a while. There were two main concerns in her mind. The first, despite her recent arrival on the Ile de Batz, was that she hadn't yet really had a conversation with anyone. The second was that it didn't bother her enough.

Though Casey had never been the life of the party, she had always enjoyed meeting and exploring people. She had needed to feel that intellectual contact in order to ground herself outside the four walls of her classroom. She wasn't sure when she'd gone from being a frequent guest at dinners and other events to being a hermit. She tried to muster a mental picture of herself as a Hermit Crab, but couldn't conceive of a shell. The analogy was inaccurate: she wasn't protectively hiding away in a safe, impenetrable place. If she were forced to compare herself to a sea-creature, it would have to be a starfish like the one she'd seen in the harbor yesterday—washed up on the edges of a tidal pool, its life suspended by ebbs and flows it couldn't control, spread eagled, helpless, and drying up under a merciless sun. In her brief journeys outside her island home, she had felt that vulnerable, unbearably exposed to the scrutiny and censure of the islanders.

She should have been angry—or at least bothered by their deliberate avoidance and uncivil behavior. She'd been either pointedly ignored or rudely dismissed by every person she had met since her arrival. *Nearly* every person. Luke and Pierrot stood out as unwitting exceptions. But the rudeness of the islanders, far from provoking the indignation it deserved, seemed just another blip on a radar that had ceased to matter.

Casey wondered when the passionate advocate of justice she once was had surrendered her weapons and meekly joined the ranks of the debilitated and despondent. There had been a time when she would have marched herself down to the gate and engaged the fish-lady so confidently and doggedly that she would have *had* to respond. Her response might have been obscene, but at least it would have been communication! But the new Casey, the Casey who wanted nothing and needed no one, lived her life like a perpetual parenthesis, a disenfranchised space between consciousness and oblivion where relentless ghosts imposed insufferable guilt on their reluctant hosts.

Nothing mattered.
Nothing.

"Auntie Casey, can we watch Nemo now?"

Five-year old Toby had the tenacity of a mule. Casey lifted her head off the pillows propping her up in bed and attempted a smile.

"Not right now, buddy. Maybe after I rest for a while."

"But…"

"*Later*, Toby," Casey repeated a little more firmly than she had intended.

Toby crossed his chubby, short arms and stuck out his bottom lip. Standing next to her little brother with the DVD in her hand, Melissa looked crestfallen.

"But Auntie Casey, you said you'd watch it with us after lunch." She was a slight child with huge blue eyes. At that moment they reflected her utter incomprehension. Grown-ups weren't supposed to break promises. Certainly not when they'd already made the same promise three days in a row. "You said today for sure," she added, her disappointment obvious in the droop of her shoulders.

"Yeah," Toby agreed, his arms still crossed and his eyebrows drawn together in an unhappy frown. "Today. You said today."

Casey sighed and rubbed her temples. "And if we watch it later this afternoon," she said carefully, tension lending a hard edge to her voice, "it will still be today."

"But you said after lunch," Toby insisted. "You said it. I heard you."

"Well, I didn't know then that I'd have a headache."

"You *always* have headaches," came Melissa's melancholic voice, almost too quietly for Casey to hear.

"Melissa..." Her niece's disheartened expression and Toby's heartfelt protestations made Casey want to relent, but she simply didn't have the energy to watch a movie. Or read a book. Or leaf through a magazine. Or help Layle clean up the kitchen. Or engage Troy in conversation. Or tidy up three-weeks worth of disorder in the guest room where she lived twenty hours a day. She just couldn't do it.

"It's okay," Melissa said quietly, valiantly trying to mask her disappointment. She held the DVD against her stomach and left the room with her head low. Toby leveled an accusatory look at Casey and followed his sister from the room, all the defiance a five-year old could muster in the rigid line of his back.

Casey looked out the window until she sensed Layle's presence. She stood in the doorway, her eyes on her sister. Casey sighed and braced herself. This moment had been a long time coming.

"You heard?" Casey asked.
"I heard."

Casey let her head fall back against the pillows and looked out the window again.

"You know what I'm going to say, right?" Layle's voice was gentle but determined.

Casey nodded. "I can't keep making promises I'm not going to keep."

"No, that's not it."

"I've been hanging around your neck like a dead weight for too long and it's time for me to start doing something to earn my keep."

"No."

Casey hesitated. She thought back to her behavior during the past few weeks and couldn't blame Layle for taking a stand. She had every right. But Casey wasn't prepared to move back to her place yet. She wasn't capable of it. "You want me to move home," she finally said, voicing the thought that overwhelmed her with impossibility.

"Casey," Layle said with genuine dismay, "I would *never* tell you to go home!"

"You should." There was no denying it.

Layle came to sit on the edge of the bed. She rested a hand on either side of Casey and looked her straight in the eyes. "You are family. You belong here. No one, absolutely *no one*, is going to tell you to leave."

Casey wasn't sure how to react. Reacting hadn't been much of a forte lately. Most of the time she didn't react at all. On the rare occasions when she did, she discovered that her reaction was either out of proportion or out of context with whatever had caused it. Since she couldn't predict her own behavior, she merely stared back at Layle, remorse and helplessness in her gaze.

"Troy and I would like you to see someone. He's an associate pastor at our church." Casey was already shaking her head. "Wait. Don't decide yet. We'd just like for you to meet with him once."

"Layle…"

"Just once, Case. That's all I ask. And then it'll be up to you."

Casey turned her head back to the window. Being told to move out would have been easier to deal with.

"This isn't you," Layle continued. "This person who hides away in here, who gets lost in thought for hours at a time, who makes promises to the kids that she doesn't keep... Case, it's just not you."

"The kids hate me," Casey said. The statement wounded her, yet she knew she had deserved their rejection.

"What?" Layle asked with a smile. "You've always been their favorite aunt—nothing's going to change that."

Casey didn't believe her.

"They're *children*," Layle continued. "They bounce back. Besides, anyone who's lived with me when I have PMS is bulletproof." She touched Casey's arm and felt her flinch. "Don't worry about them. They love you."

Casey's eyes vaguely followed the antics of a squirrel in the tree outside her window. His exuberance exhausted her. "I'll see him once," she finally conceded, unwilling to meet her sister's gaze.

Layle's voice was soft with relief. "You will?"

Casey turned her head and tried to smile. "Hey, I've lived through PMS with you too. The shrink will be a breeze."

"He's not a shrink."

"He'll be a breeze."

There was a moment of silence while the sisters exchanged wordless confessions, pains, and promises.

"I'll make the call," Layle said.

Casey would have been happy to light a fire in the fireplace, pull up the leather armchair, and spend the day immobile, gazing into the flames. But there were two problems with that plan: although she'd spent countless hours sitting by her gas fire at home, she had no idea how to light a real fire, and having flown across the world to make it to this island, she felt it was her duty to get out and explore it.

Besides, one of the things she had forgotten to pick up at the store was coffee, and with jetlag weighing her down, it was a luxury she couldn't do without. A glance out the window revealed gray skies and a persistent wind. She layered a rose-colored turtleneck and cardigan over chocolate brown corduroy pants, grabbed the jacket she'd worn for her arrival on the island, and headed up the hill toward the store. She was passing the semaphore when a better idea struck her. Why buy instant coffee when there had to be places on the island where she could buy a steaming cup of the real thing?

The only restaurant she had seen was the one down by the harbor, so she retraced her steps, giving the shrilling fish-lady a wide berth—not that she would notice—and headed toward the road lining the harbor. She smiled politely at the handful of tourists she saw and was gratified by their return greetings. As for the islanders, two older women actually crossed the street to avoid closer contact with Casey. She studiously avoided looking their way and walked on.

Casey found Pierrot sitting on a low stone wall by the harbor, a large sandwich in his hand and a beer bottle beside him. He saw her coming and his face lit up. He put his sandwich down next to his beer bottle—alarmingly close to a seagull's "mark" on the wall—and, brushing his hands on his filthy jeans, hurried over to Casey.

She was so surprised that someone on the island had actually acknowledged her presence that she took a step back and looked at him suspiciously. He was oblivious to her discomfort and came to a stop right in front of her, shoving his hands deep into low-slung pockets.

"So you're still here, huh?" he asked, although it was more of a statement than a question. His French was roughened by the *Breton* accent. It leant consonants a more guttural sound and served to make the speaker sound less educated and coarser.

Casey wasn't sure what he meant by his question. "Did you expect me to be gone already?" she asked in French.

His shoulders bounced as he smiled widely, showing off a set of teeth in desperate need of a dentist.

"You're just not the type to stick around the island, that's all. People like you just come for a day and then hightail it back to civilization. But you had a lot of suitcases, so I guess… Yeah." He had apparently run out of words and stood there nodding at nothing.

Casey was nonplussed. "People like me?"

"Yeah," he said, spitting on the ground next to his well-worn boots. He smiled and dramatically said, "*Les américains!* We love their money, but they're a bunch of wusses."

Casey wasn't sure whether to be offended by the generalization or amused by the source of the comment. At a loss, she settled for officializing her contact with this strange young man and extended a hand.

"I'm Casey," she said.

Pierrot took a hand from his pocket, wiped it on his jeans, and shook hands with her. "Pierrot," he said, looking around sheepishly as he hurriedly stuffed his hand back into his pocket. A faint blush colored his cheekbones, though Casey wasn't sure if embarrassment or pleasure had caused it.

"Do you live on the Ile de Batz?" she asked, subconsciously expecting Pierrot to turn and run at any moment.

"Uh. Yeah. I guess."

"You guess?"

He laughed nervously and aimed an awkward wave at a fisherman pulling his cart down the street. Once the sound of the cart had faded, he directed his attention back to Casey.

"I used to live in Morlaix," he said. "Now I live here."

Casey wanted to know more. Where were his parents? Where did he live on the island? How much time did he spend loitering around the harbor as he had been every time she'd seen him since her arrival?

"So," she said lightly, "what brought you here from Morlaix?"

Pierrot's shoulders rose to ear-level and stayed there while his eyebrows arched and his eyes looked sideways. "Stuff," he finally said, letting his shoulders fall. "My *Pappy* lives here."

So he had a grandfather on the island. Casey didn't know how much more to ask. This being her only precarious connection with an islander, she didn't want to jeopardize it by asking too much too soon.

"I need coffee," she finally said, bringing the conversation back to less personal topics.

A panic-stricken look crossed Pierrot's face and he took a step back.

"*Non, non!*" she hurried to add. "I'm not asking you to have coffee with me." Pierrot's relief was obvious and instantaneous. "I'm just wondering if you can tell me where to get one."

He nodded vigorously and pointed with a dirty finger toward the building he had entered with Luke the day before.

"Do they make good coffee?" Casey asked.

He nodded. "Yup. And good *crêpes* too."

"And they serve in the middle of the afternoon?" Casey asked, unwilling to face being turned back at the door.

"Oh, yeah," Pierrot answered confidently. "Marguerite is there all day and then the boss takes over."

Casey could feel her body anticipating the caffeine kick and braced herself to enter enemy territory.

"But don't get the espresso," Pierrot advised her. "It'll rot your intestines."

Casey raised a dubious eyebrow. "Really."

"Yep. That's what my *Pappy* says. But he drinks it anyway."

Pierrot looked up in the direction of approaching teenage voices. Two young ladies in tight-fitting clothes and open, oversized jackets were walking toward them on the harbor road. The boy suddenly turned fidgety, his eyes nervously darting from

Casey to the girls. Casey didn't want to put him in an awkward position, so she quickly thanked him for the information.

"It was nice to meet you," she said.

Pierrot, still frantic, had his gaze locked on the approaching girls. "Yeah," he said absently, "you too."

As Casey took a few steps toward the restaurant, she watched Pierrot rush across the street and retrieve his sandwich and beer. He then trotted back across the street and up a small road leading away from the harbor.

Casey stopped and stared at the place they had stood. She had assumed that Pierrot's anxiety was motivated by the excitement of meeting up with the girls. She now understood that it had been outright fear. He didn't want to be anywhere near the pretty girls making their way toward Casey. And he had said Americans were wusses.

Casey continued on toward the restaurant, her steps lightened by her unexpected encounter with the quirky young man. She had gleaned some valuable information from their brief conversation. Americans weren't expected to stay on the island more than a day or two. This was an ominous revelation. Would she earn their reluctant respect if she survived longer than the average, or would they hold it against her if she stayed on as a long-term, unwanted guest?

But there were more important things on Casey's mind at that moment. Despite Louise's miracle jetlag remedy, she still desperately needed caffeine. She accelerated her pace and quickly reached the front door of the restaurant. A handwritten sign in the window proclaimed that it was "*Ouvert*", but the lack of activity made her wonder if it was truly open for business.

She pushed open the turquoise door, so typical of island colors, and entered the dimly lit dining room.

"*Oui, madame?*"

A wiry woman who appeared to be in her mid-forties materialized in front of Casey. Her features were stark, her cheek bones prominent. She wore heavy eyeliner around piercing eyes.

Her expression wasn't amicable. This was a woman doing her duty despite personal reticence.

"Is it possible to have a *café au lait*?" Casey inquired in the kindest way possible.

The waitress, who Casey assumed to be Marguerite, looked pointedly at her watch.

"A young man—Pierrot—told me you served all afternoon."

Marguerite pursed her lips and gave Casey a slow once-over. Then she curtly pointed her chin in the direction of a table and headed toward the bar at the far end of the restaurant.

"*Sucre?*" she asked.

"Yes, please," Casey answered, taking a seat at the table nearest a window. "Two cubes, please."

An ironic smile briefly altered the woman's hard expression, but Casey was sure it was a "spoiled American" statement rather than a thaw in the ethnocentric chill that seemed to be a main feature of the island's mentality. Casey shrugged out of her jacket and rested her chin on her clasped hands, her elbows feeling the imprint of breadcrumbs on the table-top. She looked around the dark restaurant, taking in the handcrafted furniture, the pottery hanging on the walls, and the framed, antique prints of ships, buildings, and previous generations of islanders dressed in *Bretagne*'s traditional costumes. Casey knew from her years of study of the French culture that each region of France had its own lore, superstitions, and vestments. Brittany's traditional garb included elaborate lace headdresses, floor-length dark dresses with embroidered trim, and starched matching aprons. Casey was leaning forward, squinting in the poorly lit interior at one of the prints, when Marguerite plunked a bowl of *café au lait* in front of her. The half-milk, half-coffee mixture sloshed in the bowl and spilled out onto the table, but Marguerite paid it no attention. She stood austerely by Casey's side and demanded immediate payment.

"Six euros," she said.

Casey dutifully reached for her wallet, then stopped short when the price registered in her mind. "Six euros?" she repeated incredulously. Who paid seven dollars for a bowl of coffee?

Marguerite didn't bother to answer Casey's question. She stood by the table with one hand on her hip and waited impatiently for *l'américaine* to cough up the money. Despite her better judgment, Casey handed over a ten euro bill, which Marguerite pocketed, not bothering to give her four euros in change.

At a loss, Casey sat there and watched Marguerite walk away, unable to formulate a protest. When she looked down at her coffee and saw that the waitress had left no sugar, she found the courage to ask for it.

"Could I have two sugars?" she called before Marguerite disappeared completely into the kitchen. The woman stopped dead in her tracks for a moment, then moved with ominous slowness to the bar. She approached Casey's table again, dropped a cube of sugar next to her bowl of coffee, leveled a cold gaze at her American patron, and headed back to the kitchen.

Casey stared at the single cube of sugar next to her cup and briefly considered getting up and leaving. But she had just paid over ten dollars for her beverage and she refused to let Marguerite's antipathy drive her from her hard-earned *café au lait*. She would stay right there and take her time drinking, even if it meant Marguerite would have to remain in exile in her kitchen for the rest of the afternoon. Pierrot had said the restaurant served all day, and Casey had studied the French culture enough to know that spending an hour or two sipping a drink was simply part of the French lifestyle. She'd stay put until she was good and ready to leave.

Casey had been in the staff room drinking her habitual mid-morning coffee when Marilyn bustled in.

"Figured you'd be here," she said.

"Like clockwork. Want some coffee?"

Marilyn shook her head. "I'm just dropping off the mail. Can't be gone from the front desk too long—just in case something actually happens and I miss it when it does. Tell me again why I'm not working for Donald Trump?"

"Because you're too good for him."

"I think it's because my hair looks worse than his and he couldn't handle the competition."

Casey laughed and eyed the papers and envelopes Marilyn was putting in the teacher's boxes. "Anything there for me?"

Marilyn glanced through the papers she still held. "As a matter of fact..." she said, holding up a folded sheet of paper.

"Lucky me," Casey said sarcastically. "Looks like an overdue assignment. I love it when they're too cowardly to hand them in face-to-face."

"Uh-huh," Marilyn agreed. "You've just *got* to love the little scoundrels."

"The little *devils*."

Marilyn thought hard and came up with a better definition. "The little turds," she said.

"Marilyn!"

"What? I get to see the real deal when they get hauled in to the principal's office. It ain't pretty, I'm telling you."

"Well, maybe I just have the sweet ones in my classes."

Marilyn was almost finished with her distribution. "It's pretty hard to sound rebellious if you're in a class where you have to talk like Pepe Le Pew," she said, getting rid of one last envelope with a flourish. "Here's yours," she said, dropping the folded paper with Casey's name on it into her lap. "See you after school? We can look up Tajikistan together on the Internet."

"Already done," Casey answered, "but I might drop by just for the company."

"Oh, puh-shaw," Marilyn said with a dismissive wave, "flattery will get you no free photocopying, young lady."

After Marilyn left the teacher's lounge, Casey picked up the paper she had delivered and unfolded it. She immediately recognized Ben's sharp penmanship. His writing was narrow, tall, and angular. At the top of the page were three words: *Three Basic Statements*. Her curiosity piqued, she read the short statements Ben had made, each numbered and carefully printed.

*1. If god can't be seen or touched or heard, how does he expect intelligent people to believe he's really out there? And what makes him any different from Santa Claus or the tooth fairy?*

*2. There are millions of christians in the world, but I haven't seen them making much of a dent in the bad stuff out there. There are still wars and murders and atrocities. Some of them against believers and some of them BY believers. So what good does it do to "know god"?*

*All the christians I know have this narrow-minded opinion that everyone who believes differently from them is wrong. How can god promote that kind of intolerance? As far as I know, the bible says to love the sinners, but the christians I've seen just try to indoctrinate them. They might think they know the REAL truth, but what gives them the right to impose it on others?*

*3. It seems like the only scientists who have proved that jesus really existed already believed in him anyway. So it's pretty tough to accept their point of view when it's probably biased. For every christian who proves jesus' existence there are ten atheists who disprove it. The majority vote usually wins, right?*

*Miss Jensen, I hope you don't think I'm insulting you. Just wanted to do your "assignment" in an honest way. Hope you're not offended…*

*B.*

Casey reread the page several times before putting it down. Then she reached for her cup and, propping her feet on the coffee table in front of her chair, considered Ben's request for proof and her own inability to provide it. Casey knew that faith was not a cookie-cutter phenomenon exactly replicated in each person who believes. A mathematician would describe his faith in completely different terms than an artist would use. Both would be accurate, just perceived differently. She tended to define her faith as the artist would: in instinctive beliefs, intuitions, and unwavering assurance, regardless of tangible or scientific proofs. She just *knew*. But there was no explaining that to a mind like Ben's without risking his immediate dismissal. He was looking for an equation that would prove God's existence. He wanted a street address where he could meet Him or a miracle that would prove beyond a doubt that He was real. Ben wanted the opposite of faith, and Casey wasn't sure how to point that out to him without sounding simplistic.

She gave it a few minutes of thought, then decided these questions were too vital to be put off. She found a pen and quickly scribbled her response under his words and on the flip side of the page.

*Ben, thanks for the "assignment"!*

*1. The fact that God can't be seen or touched is exactly why faith is required. Faith is based on two major things: what you know and what you don't know. The facts related through the accounts of those who know God (historically and currently) or were contemporaries of His Son are valid "support beams". The rest of faith rests on those truths, but it requires that you stop trying to prove a negative and start believing in a positive. The latter takes a lot more faith, but yields infinitely more satisfaction.*

*2. The problem with Christianity in action is that it requires more than just wishful thinking. History proves that Christianity has indeed made a positive difference, either on a large or a small scale, but only when believers were committed to bettering the world, determined in their endeavors and compassionate in their approach. If you're familiar with the Bible's teachings, you'll realize that those who have harmed others were in contradiction to its teachings, and those who have enriched the lives of others were in line with God's commands.*

*The problem is that humans are imperfect, and though our hearts might be in the right place, we're often sidetracked or misled by our own agendas. You're absolutely right in saying that those of us who hate people because of their beliefs or their differences are patently in opposition to God's teaching. We can disagree with the faiths of others and we can stand in opposition to injustice and immorality without making it a vicious attack on a person. But as you inventory the Christians who strike you as hypocritical or abusive, please also note that many of us are truly trying to love others, even if we do so poorly at times.*

*3. Intelligence needn't be surrendered in order to embrace faith. Doubt should be. Sir Francis Bacon said, "A little science estranges a man from God. A lot of science brings him back." Scientists who are out to disprove God will eventually find shreds of evidence that support their point. The same goes for scientists who try to prove him. But I suggest you research some of the world's most intelligent minds who questioned Christianity and God's goodness, but ended up embracing both almost in spite of themselves and despite the questions they still couldn't answer. If those brilliant intellects were swayed by evidence and instinct, their findings must be respected. I suggest the works of C.S. Lewis as a starting point. Also see writings by St. Augustine, Francis of Assisi, Thomas Aquinas, and Soren Kierkegaard for examples of some of the world's most intelligent men and their understanding of what Christianity is truly about.*

*That's all I'll write for now. Maybe we can discuss this again some time? Your intelligence and inquisitiveness surpass your years, Ben, and that can truly be a burden. Please understand that though you want to prove everything beyond a doubt, some of who God is and how He works just can't be grasped, even by your brilliant mind.*

*Miss Jensen*

## *Chapter Five*

Casey had been idly sitting at the table in the restaurant for an hour when Marguerite emerged from the kitchen and approached her table. Though Marguerite was not a large woman, Casey half expected to feel tremors in the floor with every step she took toward her, so formidable was her presence. Marguerite stood by the table in complete silence. Casey sat gazing at a spot on the wall across from her just as silently.

"Another coffee," Marguerite finally said. It was a statement—the farthest thing from a question.

Casey took a breath and clung to her resolve. "No, thank you," she said, smiling politely—if not sincerely—at Marguerite.

"You can't just sit here and not drink."

"I'm not quite finished with my *café au lait*."

"It's cold."

"I don't mind."

"You can't just sit here," she repeated, more firmly this time.

During the hour Casey had sat there, the door of the restaurant had opened several times and customers had entered. But they had only stayed long enough to notice Casey sitting at the table. Once they'd seen her there, they had left as quickly as they'd come. She entertained herself by cataloguing their expressions as they departed. Some looked angry, others looked frustrated, and some wore an expression that was equal parts surprise and disapproval. All looked at Casey only until they recognized her, and though some began an instinctive greeting, none of them completed it. From the moment they registered who she was, she became invisible.

It amazed Casey that so many islanders, most of whom had never seen her, recognized her so easily. How did they know about *l'américaine* who had taken up residence on their island? How had word spread and what had the word been? What was it she had done that was so unanimously censured? From the moment she had left the Roscoff pier, she had been shown nothing but scorn. Something unfamiliar had stirred inside her, minutes before, when the last islander had rolled his eyes at her and exited the restaurant. It was the same flutter of energy Marguerite's presence next to her table evoked.

"You shouldn't be here."

Casey looked directly at her hostess. "I'm a paying customer."

"I mean on the island. You don't belong here."

Casey felt the burn of adrenalin traveling through her limbs. This went beyond rudeness. It was an outright attack. She thought for a moment about standing her ground and confronting Marguerite. She wanted to resist and knew she should, yet everything she'd endured in the previous months demanded that she run, that she cower, that she withdraw. The courage it had taken for her to enter the restaurant had been spent, and that small victory seemed voided by her inability to defend herself against Marguerite's relentless attacks.

So Casey stood, lifted her coat off the back of her chair, and left the restaurant in as dignified a manner as she could while her mind reeled and her body shook from the brutality of Marguerite's treatment. Her words had had the effect of a physical blow, and Casey felt their sting as she walked home, opened the door of her house and dropped to the floor in front of the leather chair. She could have sat *in* the chair, but the internal voice she'd been obeying since mid-August told her she didn't deserve its comfort. That same voice had convinced her of other forbidden luxuries: lightness of being, friendship, and connection. She didn't deserve any of them.

Casey sat on the floor by her empty fireplace and willed herself to go numb. If she could just eliminate emotions from her mind. Anger, frustration, indignation, humiliation. She felt them sink into a deeper space and, out of sight, spread warmly into a physical paralysis. There was something comforting about the lethargy that stole into her mind and deadened it. An invisible weight immobilized her body and made effort pointless. This was her reality, the new-normal she had accepted without a fight. Equally brutal and salutary, this half-death was her survival.

∞

Pastor Scott, as he preferred to be called, was a tall man with thinning blonde hair, stylish glasses, and a winning smile. He sauntered into the office just a few seconds after his secretary had escorted Casey in.

"Casey?" he asked, stretching out his hand in greeting.

She stood to shake it.

"Have you been waiting long?" He strode to his desk and put his briefcase down beside it, then moved to sit in an armchair, motioning for Casey to sit on the couch from which she'd just risen.

"Just a couple minutes," she answered, trying to look confident despite the nervousness churning in her stomach. "I'm here because my sister wanted me to come," she said, not sure what had prompted her to make the revelation. Maybe she just didn't want him to expect too much from her. Layle had asked that she see him, and she owed her this much. But she had made no further promises.

Pastor Scott chuckled and settled in to his chair. "So you're here under duress," he said.

Casey nodded.

"And the reason you didn't want to come is…?" He left the question dangling.

Casey simply stared at him. She had grown accustomed to the near impossibility of formulating a coherent thought, but losing her cognitive powers in a situation like this was more embarrassing than in the solitude of her own room. The formality of the setting and her reticence to be there had combined to dramatically increase the static in her mind.

"Casey?"

She knew an answer was required. *Shut up, shut up, shut up,* she commanded the chaos in her mind. But there was no hushing it. Not this time. It was as if the turmoil had taken on a life of its own and was clamoring to be heard.

"Casey?"

She realized she had been staring at Pastor Scott, and, from his reaction, assumed that her expression must have reflected her panic.

"I'm sorry," she said hurriedly, clasping her hands tightly in her lap. "I'm just not used to this type of thing." *Be still,* she commanded herself.

"Do you need to take a moment?" Pastor Scott's voice was gentle, his offer sincere.

"No. Thank you." She let out a deep breath. "I'm okay. Just a little out of practice talking!" She attempted a light laugh.

"So you haven't been talking," he said. He had a gentle manner that seemed more sympathetic than analytical.

The static in Casey's mind picked up a notch, but she fought it back. "No, I've been talking," she said, trying to minimize the situation. "Just not like this. Not with questions…and stuff." She knew she wasn't making much sense. She was a teacher. She should know how to interact in a more formal setting like this one. She should be able to predict his next question and have an answer formed by the time he asked it. But simple as they were, his questions so far had felt like tests of momentous importance.

"Can you tell me why you didn't want to come here today?" It was the second time he had asked the question, and her mind's response was to slip toward incoherence again.

"Can you ask me another question?" she asked before the mental anarchy took over. She knew her question was ridiculous and her behavior erratic, but she had the terrifying feeling that something horrible would happen if she failed this test.

"Sure," Pastor Scott said, shifting in his chair to rest his elbows on his knees and stare more closely at his patient. "Maybe it would be easier for you to tell me why your sister wanted you to see me."

He was right. It was an easier question to answer. Possibly because it didn't directly involve her own thoughts and emotions.

"She's concerned about me. I… Well, haven't quite been myself for a while." She smiled, but the smile was far from cheerful. "She's hoping you can fix me."

"Do you live with your sister?"

"I have since the beginning of September."

"And is this a long-term arrangement?"

Casey shook her head. "I have my own home. In Glen Ellyn."

"How is it living with Layle and her family?" he asked.

There were too many answers to that question. Or maybe not enough.

"Casey?"

She looked up, startled. "It's…" She hesitated. "It's okay. I guess."

Pastor Scott sat back in his chair and steepled his fingers. He stared at Casey long enough to arouse the white noise in her mind again. She closed her eyes against the cacophony.

Pastor Scott's voice came from far away. "Casey, tell me why you moved in with your sister in September. What happened in your life that made you move out of your home and in with your relatives?" His words were softly spoken, his tone at once comforting and inquiring.

Casey felt a familiar burn go down her spine. For the past two months, her life had alternated between the unintelligible chaos that sent her to the edge of panic and this numbing heat that usually followed the chaos and seemed to paralyze her lungs.

"I'm not answering that question," she said.

"It would help me to know what happened to make you move… "

"I'm not answering that question," she repeated, meeting his gaze, at once imploring and commanding him to stop. She couldn't go there. She wouldn't.

She felt the predictable mutation of searing heat into frantic fear. She hadn't been able to withdraw from Pastor Scott's scrutiny as she had learned to do when her mind spun out of control. She had had to sit there and endure his questions. And now she felt the mobile panic in her gut, the wild recklessness of untamable terror that made her want to stand and scream and suffer physical pain before the horror inside her tore her to pitiable shreds.

Casey's purse fell from her lap as she stood and stumbled toward the door. Pastor Scott said her name a couple times and instructed his secretary to call Layle as he followed his patient from his office. Casey was aware of long hallways, of doors standing in her way, of guttural sounds as she pushed through them and staggered into the painful sunlight. She thought she heard Pastor Scott instructing her to give him her keys, telling her she wasn't in a state to drive. She shook off his grip on her arm, climbed into her car, and heard him slapping her car windows with his palms as she drove out of the parking lot.

Later, she would remember driving slowly—too slowly—so scared of hurting someone again. *No more. No more. No more.* The chill descended—again. Numbed again. Deadened again. Casey embraced the relief.

Layle was waiting at the curb when Casey turned into her street. Her face was pale, her body rigid. She opened the driver-side door before Casey had even come to a halt.

"Case," she whispered desperately, helping her sister from the car and wrapping her in a ferocious embrace.

But the strain had been too much for Casey's body to endure. She pushed out of her sister's arms and staggered toward the tree shading her front yard. She retched until her legs gave out and her arms clung to the rough bark for support. She was aware of her sister's hands under her elbows, of her comforting words. They walked inside together, went straight to Casey's room. Layle helped her out of her shoes, pulled back the sheets, and tucked her into bed. Casey turned her face toward the wall and closed her eyes.

*Shut up. Shut up. Shut up.*
The chill took over.

Darkness had enveloped the island again. Casey had sat through dusk without noticing that it had come and gone. The dampness of the cold draft blowing in around loose window frames finally brought her back to reality.

She stared into the fireplace and wondered if it was safe to light a fire. There were several logs in a wicker carrier next to the step that surrounded the wide, brick-framed hearth. Judging by the bark falling off the wood, it was dry and eager to burn. Casey grunted a little as she pulled herself up off the floor, using the leather chair for leverage. She stretched sore muscles as she went to the kitchen to retrieve a book of matches and anything she could find in Louise's recycling box to use as kindling. Returning to the living room with cardboard cereal boxes under her arm, she began to tear them into smaller pieces, making a precarious pile on the floor of the fireplace. She topped the pile with pieces of bark and topped that layer with the smallest logs in the stack. A last-minute misgiving made her double-check that the flue was open. She struck a match and lit the cardboard. It wasn't long before the cardboard and bark were alight with yellow and blue flames, sparks shooting harmlessly from dried wood and landing on the brick threshold of the fireplace. Some smoke wafted into the room, but Casey figured that it would be drawn up the chimney just as soon as the flames were hot enough. She allowed herself to climb into the armchair and curled up, fascinated, as she had always been, by the indomitable progress of fire. She watched the small logs catch and burn, waiting until they were partially consumed before she added larger logs on top of them.

She wasn't sure how long she'd been sitting there observing the flames when she became aware of an unusual sound. Although the fire was burning well, the sound it was making seemed completely out of proportion with the flames. Alarmed, Casey rose and stepped closer, realizing that the sound was coming not from the fireplace, but from a much higher part of the chimney. She'd heard enough about chimney fires to know she was in trouble.

With no phone in the house to call for help, she became frantic. She ran to the kitchen and began to fill a pot with water, but the process was agonizingly slow. Grabbing a pitcher of iced-tea she had made the day before, she rushed back to the living room and only partially extinguished the flames with the limited amount of liquid. But she knew the danger wasn't in the fire in the hearth; it was far above her head where layers of deposit had caught fire and were burning out of control. If she couldn't extinguish the flames quickly, there was a very real danger of the entire house burning down. Running back to the kitchen with panic weighing down her legs and adrenalin heightening her senses, she grabbed the nearly-full pot of water from the sink and headed back to the living room, wondering as she went which neighbor she could run to if this last effort didn't help. The house to the left of hers was uninhabited and probably just a summer home. She had never met the people who lived in the hedge-rimmed house to the right of hers.

She threw the water on the flames and watched it bubble and steam as it connected with the logs. Though they were no longer on fire, the raging sound in the chimney above them had not diminished.

"Oh God, oh God, oh *God*!" Casey moaned, truly begging for divine intervention, the immediate danger pushing her to seek help from a source she hadn't so much as considered for months. A familiar cacophony filled her mind, rendering her powerless. She stared in utter horror up toward the ceiling and continued to beg internally for a miracle.

The sound of her front door slamming back on its hinges snapped Casey out of her panicked trance. She turned to see Luke striding quickly into her living room. Relief flooded her body.

"I… I don't know what to do," she rasped, fear having robbed her voice of all but a whisper.

But Luke wasn't listening. He went straight to the fireplace and searched its mantel for something he didn't find. He roughly pulled open the drawers of the buffet, leaving each dangling as he moved on to the next. He finally strode to the wicker wood carrier by the fireplace and threw it out of the way, finding what looked like a large red road flare behind it. He struck it twice and let the combustion grow for just a moment before tossing it into the fireplace, right under the chimney. Thick fumes ascended out of sight.

"You have a water hose?" he asked gruffly as he strode back out of the living room and toward the front door.

"Uhm…" Casey was frantic. "I don't know!" she called. But he had already left. She rushed to the front door and saw his form disappearing around the side of the house. He reappeared a moment later.

"Where is the main water valve for the garden hose?"

Again, Casey knew too little and was too distraught to answer. "I don't *know*," she admitted as he brushed past her and entered the house. He headed straight for the kitchen, pulled open the cabinet beneath the sink, and found a large copper tap next to the sink's drainpipe. Once he had turned it to its full-open position, he went back outside with a curt, "Stay in the living room and make sure nothing's falling out of the chimney."

She immediately realized the danger and hurried into the living room. The torch still released thick smoke in the fireplace, and the raging in the chimney had decreased considerably. When she'd ascertained that nothing was falling from the inside of the chimney and threatening to start a fire on the living room floor, she headed outside and found Luke standing with a water hose aimed at the roof,

"I think the fire is out," Casey said hesitantly, her eyes wide with panic even after the danger had passed. She marveled that she was able to form coherent sentences in French under such circumstances, then wondered if she'd been speaking French at all.

He nodded. "The chimney is still hot enough to set the roof on fire," he said, explaining the hose and the water he was aiming at the shingles surrounding the chimney.

Casey put out a hand to steady herself against the wall. She looked up at the windows in the house across the way and saw heads furtively pulling back. An arm reached out and pulled the shutters closed. They had seen the fire but had done nothing to help. She stared in stricken disbelief.

Luke's eyes went from her pale face to the neighbor's house, then back to Casey.

"You should go inside," he said.

"Can I help you?" It was a softly spoken plea.

His gaze was unwavering and direct. "Go inside," he repeated.

Casey obediently turned to go, but her legs buckled. She felt Luke's hand under her elbow, holding her up until she was steady again. Then, her hand trailing against the wall for support, she made her way through the dark to her front door.

Luke found her leaning against the doorjamb into the living room when he entered minutes later wiping cold, wet hands on his jeans.

She started when he spoke. "I think it'll be alright." When she put a hand to her throat, he added, "I'm sorry. Didn't mean to startle you."

"That's okay," she answered, her voice still hoarse, her eyes still wide and fearful. "What…" There were too many questions. "Is the roof okay?"

He nodded, his wide-set, piercing eyes looking right at her. Even in her distraught state of mind, she found their blueness remarkable. "We got it early," he said.

"*You* got it early," Casey amended, the hand at her throat shaking as she realized what could have happened. "I didn't know what to do."

His mouth tilted a bit into a near-smile. "That much was obvious."

Casey shook her head in confusion, not sure whether to be insulted by his comment. But the not-quite-there smile seemed genuine and the statement was more honest than mocking.

"What made you…?"

He seemed amused by her inability to finish a sentence. *Stick around*, she thought sadly, *this is only the tip of the iceberg*.

He guessed the rest of her question and answered in his soft, nearly expressionless voice. "I was walking home and saw the flames in your chimney."

"I could have burned the house down," Casey said, retroactive horror in her voice. He said nothing. He just stood there, his unflinching gaze answering her statement. She vaguely realized that he was younger than she'd thought. In his mid-thirties. His dark, wavy hair was shaggy and badly in need of a cut, and his tan, weathered face needed a shave. But there was something in his quiet stance and steady gaze that suggested dignity and confidence.

Casey looked around the room at the drawers still hanging from the buffet and pointed with a shaky hand toward the overturned wood carrier. "How did you know…?"

He shrugged. "Everybody here has an extinguisher. I figured it had to be in this room somewhere." He turned and headed toward the front door, buttoning his navy blue wool jacket.

"Wait," Casey called after him.

He stopped at the door.

"How can I thank you? You saved this house. There's got to be something I can do for you."

Without turning around, he pulled a wool hat over his thick, curly hair and left her house with a quiet, "You might want to call the chimney sweep."

Then he was gone—as unexpectedly as he had come.

Casey wandered back into the living room and assessed the damage. The water she had used to put out the flames had formed ashy puddles around the base of the fireplace. Aside from that, the open drawers, and the overturned wood basket, the room was unharmed. Casey went to the window and pulled back the heavy drapes. There was no sign of Luke in the street. She realized they had never introduced themselves, and although she knew his name, she was probably just *l'américaine* to him, a lost soul who had washed up on his island without the slightest ability to take care of herself. Curiosity and embarrassment dueled in her mind. But as she locked her front door an hour later and climbed the stairs to her bedroom, she was just grateful to still have a roof over her head—and for the stranger who had spared her from having to inform Louise that she had lost her family home.

# Chapter Six

"So where did your family live before you moved back to the States, Ben?" Casey asked. They were manning the hotdog stand at the school's yearly fundraising event in which staff members and star athletes had been asked to participate. Neither she nor Ben had known until they looked at the list of assignments that they would be working together for the first two hours of the event before rotating to other positions. Ben's reaction had been somewhat skewed by the fact that he had read the list in the company of his soccer friends. They immediately began to harass him about being stuck with a female teacher, and he responded with some well-aimed verbal jabs and a couple friendly punches.

The fundraiser was a well-publicized community event that boasted of rides, games, and every form of junk food imaginable. Because it lasted all day, the number of visitors ebbed and flowed. In the middle of the morning, there were few customers at the hotdog stand, which gave Casey the opportunity to ask Ben some questions.

As Ben didn't seem inclined to answer Casey's question, she confessed to already knowing the answer.

"I've got to tell you—I checked your record and found out you lived in Tajikistan. Why would you want to hide that? It was a pretty unique experience, wasn't it?"

Ben didn't look convinced. "It was okay," he said.

"How many years were you there?"

He was struggling with his answers, knowing full well

that answering too many questions would set a dangerous precedent.

"Hey, I'm not trying to pry anything out of you," Casey assured him. "You don't have to answer any of my questions if you don't want to." She turned to stock the small fridge at the back of the stand, then thought she should clarify one thing. "*Except* in class," she added. "In that case you *absolutely* have to answer my questions!"

There was a laugh in her voice as she said it, but no answering smile on Ben's face.

"So..." she said, struggling to find a viable conversation opener. She ran through the gamut of teenage topics in her mind, but found none that seemed suited to Benjamin James Landon. Video games? Popular music? TV shows? No—she couldn't imagine that he'd have much of an opinion on those considering that most of his energies seemed to be devoted to philosophy and sports. Casey was opening her mouth to ask a banal question about World Cup Soccer when Ben's voice interrupted her.

"I was there for five years."

She was startled into immobility, then realized she'd better play it casual and keep asking questions while he was in an answering mood.

"So you moved over there when you were...?"

"Thirteen."

Casey finished stocking the fridge and turned to lean against the counter, facing Ben.

"How did you like it?"

"You probably don't even know where Tajikistan is..." His expression held disdain.

"Sure I do."

He looked at her doubtfully.

"I looked it up," she explained. He nodded and nearly smiled. "You know, just because I've never been outside the States doesn't mean I'm a *complete* moron."

He did smile at that. "I didn't say you were a moron…" His voice was flat, but his eyes held traces of unexpected mirth.

"Well, I've always been of the mind that if you insult yourself first, no one else gets the first jab," she explained, pleased to see his smile broadening. She decided to push her luck. "So tell me why your parents moved over there."

He leaned over the counter, his forearms braced on its blue surface, and casually observed the small number of visitors strolling down the aisles on the overcast, humid morning.

Casey wondered if this was his usual mode of communication rather than a deliberate mulishness—to hear the question, to think it over without giving any sign of having heard it, and then to answer when he felt like it. She decided to test her theory and let the question stand and the silence lengthen.

It only took a few seconds for his answer to come. "They were missionaries," he said, and she couldn't mistake the trace of a sneer that crossed his face.

Casey was dumbfounded. No wonder he knew so much about theology. What surprised her was that he seemed closer to being an atheist than to being a believer.

"Really," she said casually. "What kind of work did they do over there?"

She waited for the customary silence to pass.

When he spoke, the sneer she'd seen earlier had reached his voice. It was with biting sarcasm that he said, "Evangelism." He made it sound like a monumental flaw.

Casey opted to avoid spiritual topics for the time being. "And you were home-schooled because you didn't speak the language?"

"Yeah." His tone of voice reflected the distaste on his face.

She smiled. "And how much exactly did you hate it?"

This time, he didn't pause before answering. "How much would you hate having to listen to rap music six hours a day?"

Casey laughed. "That bad, huh?"

"Worse. Imagine if it was your *mom* forcing you to listen to it."

Casey laughed again, pleased to discover the lighter side of the intense young man. She wouldn't have thought that he possessed the levity for joking.

"So what's Tajikistan like?" she asked, genuinely curious about a country she'd heard mentioned only once or twice in her life.

He let a few seconds pass. "I wouldn't know," he finally said.

"You don't know?" She had trouble believing it. He'd been there for five years, after all.

"I never really went out."

"But you must have seen *something* of the country…"

Another pause. "I stayed in my room, mostly."

"In your room," she repeated.

Several seconds passed. "Yeah."

"You didn't have friends?"

He looked around as if willing someone to come to their booth and interrupt the conversation. "There wasn't really anybody around," he said.

Casey couldn't accept that. "You must have had neighbors…or coworkers' kids…or someone to hang out with."

He looked at her with something that bordered on disdain. "There wasn't anybody," he repeated. "And I wasn't interested in *hanging out*." He made her terminology sound juvenile.

Casey thought he must have been exaggerating. No teenager could live in seclusion for five years.

"Did you ever travel?" she ventured.

She waited dutifully for him to gather the energy or desire to answer.

"Not really."

"That's so sad! You could have visited places people like me will never see!"

Long pause. "My parents were busy saving the world.

They didn't have time to travel."

He looked at her then, waiting for the next words she would say and expecting her to fail this test. Casey discarded any attempts at sympathy and decided honesty was what the situation required.

"They should have made some time to go out and explore," she finally said. "How often will you have that chance again?"

Sarcasm dripped from his voice when he quickly answered, "But they were saving *souls*."

A clearer picture of Ben's relationship with faith began to form in Casey's mind. "Well, they were your parents too."

"Not after they became missionaries."

"Meaning…?"

"They were busy, that's all."

Casey wondered if he was exaggerating. "I'm sure they didn't spend *all* their time working…"

Ben stopped her words with a well-aimed glare. She wasn't sure what the emotion was, but it was powerful and sincere.

"I'm sorry, Ben," she said when no other response came to her mind.

He shrugged. "I don't really care."

"I think you do." She watched him for a moment, not sure of how far she should push her point, but keenly aware that this young man needed his pain affirmed. She finally said, "Anyone who reads the Bible knows family should come *first*. I'm sorry that wasn't the case with you."

There was no humor in Ben's laugh. He shook his head and shrugged. "Maybe they read a different Bible."

Casey suspected there was more to his story. "I'm guessing you didn't want to move to Tajikistan in the first place."

A muscle twitched in his jaw and betrayed his anger. "I had a life here."

Casey persisted. "So you didn't want to go."

He looked her square in the eye and repeated, "I had a life here."

Casey wondered what it was that kept Ben from outrightly stating his reticence to leave. Was it a feeling of loyalty to his parents? Was it an engrained belief that children shouldn't disagree with their elders, certainly not when doing God's work was involved? From what little he had revealed so far, Ben had lost everything that meant anything to him when his parents had moved to the other side of the world. Yet he couldn't bring himself to voice that in so many words.

A frazzled woman with three hyperactive children approached the hotdog stand like a castaway might approach a rescue boat.

"Three hotdogs," she begged, turning to yell at her three kids that they wouldn't get any if they didn't settle down.

"Any drinks?" Casey asked as Ben served up three hotdogs.

"Cokes," the woman answered, then quickly changed her mind. "Wait! No! No caffeine. I'll take three Sprites instead."

Casey retrieved three cans of Sprite from the fridge while the woman settled her bill with Ben. Then, yelling at the kids that there would be no more hotdogs if they dropped those, she hustled them over to a picnic table nearby for a very early lunch.

"Being a parent sucks," Ben said without prompting.

Casey didn't know how to respond. "How so?"

"Look at them," he said, cocking his head in the direction of the woman desperately trying to maintain control over her brood of overactive children. "She look happy to you?"

Casey had trouble disagreeing with him when the sound of the woman's raised voice was drawing stares all over the carnival. But she knew this was just a snapshot of the larger picture. "This is just one moment in that family's life," she told Ben, realizing her argument would fall short of persuading him. "You can't judge them by what you're seeing now. Things might be entirely different when they're not wandering around a carnival hyped up on sugar and adrenaline."

"Whatever," Ben said.

"Do you think your parents dislike being parents?" she asked, hoping the question wouldn't send Ben running.

She saw the usual sarcasm flash into his eyes before he answered. "They dislike having to deal with us when there is more important work to do."

"Us," Casey said.

"My brothers and sisters."

"How many do you have?"

"You read my file," he reminded her.

She smiled. "I just wanted to find out where you'd lived. I didn't read much more than that."

She waited for him to answer her question. He stood there in silence.

"How many of you were there?" she asked again.

"Five."

It was Casey's turn to be quiet. She had seen missionaries being paraded in front of her church all her life. They had spoken in her Sunday school classes, their children had recited verses in their adopted language, the church had had yearly drives to raise money for their special projects. But in all those years of observing missionaries, she had never considered how a move to a foreign country might have affected their children, especially if they were older. She couldn't imagine making such a dramatic change in lifestyles at any age, let alone at such a vulnerable stage of life.

"So you all moved overseas with your parents and were home-schooled by your mom?"

Ben nodded. "My sisters came back to the States though."

"When they finished high school?"

"No," Ben answered. Casey was gratified that the pause between her questions and his answers was getting shorter. "They came back after three months."

Casey knew that she was treading a fine line between asking pertinent questions and prying into areas he wasn't comfortable discussing. She was formulating her next question when Ben offered more information.

"Tajikistan isn't a great place for girls," he said.

"Were your sisters in danger?"

"Not that we knew of. It's just that they were blonde…and kind of loud."

"So your parents sent them back to the States." Casey was incredulous.

He shrugged. "It was easier that way."

She felt a flush of anger. "Easier for who?"

He shrugged again.

Casey refrained from saying any more. She knew that her own feelings about the subject wouldn't help Ben if she blurted them out in frustration. There would be time to discuss this further. But the caretaker in her rebelled at the thought that parents could take their responsibilities so lightly.

The midday crowd was arriving and the fundraiser was switching into high gear. It wouldn't be long before a line formed in front of the hotdog stand. In the last few minutes of relative inactivity, Casey asked her final questions.

"Where did your sisters live when they came back?"

"My grandparents'." His voice was gruff.

"Did they keep in touch with you?"

"Not really."

"Do they now?"

"No. They still live in South Carolina near my grandparents. They've kinda got their own thing going there."

Casey struggled to understand how his parents' ministry seemed to have destroyed the family so completely.

"Do you wish your parents hadn't gone?" she asked quietly, trying a new twist on the question he had refused to answer earlier.

"I wish they had left me in the States." It was an oblique answer.

"But then you wouldn't have been with your parents for all those years."

"I wasn't with them anyway," he interrupted her bitterly. "I might as well have been here."

*Let's hear it for the Christian family*, Casey thought, surprised at her strong reaction to Ben's story. But she was a protective person by nature, and she couldn't understand how Ben's best interests had been overlooked by those who were supposed to love him the most.

Two of Ben's soccer buddies strutted up to the hotdog stand with high-fives and attitudes.

"How's life in the estrogen zone?" one of them asked loudly enough for Casey to hear.

"It smells better and the IQ is higher," Casey answered sweetly. "And this particular female could make it *real* hard for you two wise guys to pass her French class."

They staggered back in mock injury and laughed with Casey. When she offered them two free hotdogs, they dutifully dropped a couple dollars in the donation box and promised her they'd be good for the rest of the afternoon. She took care of other customers while Ben and his friends shot the breeze, but every so often she'd remember their discussion, glance his way, and feel a physical sadness for the sensitive young man who had been so let down by the people closest to him.

After another frustrating bath/shower in her tiny bathroom, Casey spent a good part of the afternoon the day after the fire making phone calls at the post office. She wondered if she'd ever grow accustomed to the sudden silence that descended whenever she entered a public place. The handful of customers doing business on that afternoon stopped their conversations the moment she walked in and studiously avoided looking her way. There was a row of phone cubicles just inside the door, and, after buying a phone card at the booth, Casey installed herself at the phone closest to the door. The first call she made was to Layle.

"Case!" she yelled as soon as she recognized her sister's voice. "I am *so* glad to hear from you! How was your flight? What's been going on over there? Why haven't you called?"

The onslaught of questions briefly muddled Casey's mind. "In that order?" she asked.

"Uh…sure!"

"It's good to hear you too. My flight was fine, nothing much has been going on over here, and I've been busy getting moved in," she said.

Layle was a bit taken aback by the efficiency of her sister's response. "Well, do you like it there? What is the island like?"

As much as she had prepared for this question, Casey still felt ill equipped to answer it. She settled for a semi-lie that would ease her sister's concern and not be outright enough to send Casey straight to hell.

"It's interesting," she said. "Very different from Glen Ellyn."

"Is it incredibly quaint and beautiful?"

No lies needed for this one. "It really is. I think you'd like it."

"Have you met any interesting people?"

"I've met nothing *but* interesting people."

"Are they…?"

"Layle, I'm on limited time here," Casey interrupted, convinced her sister's next questions would be harder to answer.

There was a brief silence at the other end of the line. "We miss you around here, Case. The kids do too. I keep pointing France out to them on the globe in the living room, but I'm not sure they've grasped just how far it is yet."

"Tell them hi from me?"

"Sure. They'll be sorry they missed you. They're out with Troy getting some groceries."

"Are you all doing okay?" Casey asked, dutifully carrying on the requisite conversation.

"We're fine, Case. Just concerned about you. How are you holding up?"

*What—despite the fire, the general nastiness, and the missing toilet seat?*

"I'm doing fine, Layle. Don't worry about me."

She could hear her sister's grandfather clock marking the hour.

"It's hard to believe you're really over there," Layle said more quietly. "Are you sure you're okay?"

Casey sighed. Layle knew she hadn't been okay in months. "I'm hanging in, Layle." It was an honest assessment.

"Good. I'm really glad to hear that, Case."

"I should hang up. My card isn't going to last long and I have a couple more calls to make."

"Oh. Okay." Layle's voice held disappointment.

"I just wanted you to know I'd gotten here safely."

"Thank you so much, Case. I feel better now."

"Kiss the kids for me?"

She heard her sister laugh. "What, and leave Troy out? He'll be heartbroken."

"Kiss the kids and hug Troy. How's that?"

"Perfect. We miss you, Case. Really."

"Thanks, Layle. I'll call again soon."

"'kay. Love you!"

Casey hung up. She could have told her sister about the drama since her arrival on the Ile de Batz, but it only would have served to worry her more. Besides, there was nothing Layle could do about it. Casey was the only person who could hope to resolve the chimney problem and thaw relations between the islanders and herself. She knew she could call a chimney sweep for the fireplace, but the islanders were another problem altogether.

She opted to tackle the easy dilemma first.

Locating the phonebook on a shelf under the payphone, Casey flipped through it looking for the phone number of a local *ramoneur*. Not surprisingly, she found no chimney sweep listed in the index of Ile de Batz businesses—what few there were.

She looked around at the two patrons standing in line and the worker behind the desk, wondering which of the three would be most likely to give her assistance. Based on past experience, she knew "none" was the correct answer. With a deep breath and simulated confidence, Casey rose from the stool in her payphone cubicle and stepped toward the elderly gentleman standing at the back of the two-person line.

"Excuse me," she said.

He looked straight at her, which she interpreted as a good sign.

"I need to find a chimney sweep."

He stared expressionlessly.

"Do you know if there is one on the island?"

The man continued to stare through watery eyes, his face registering neither comprehension nor disdain.

"I'd be so grateful if you could give me the name of someone…"

The man put an end to his interminable stare by turning back toward the front of the line. Casey was left staring at the jagged wrinkles in his neck and the fallen lines of his face. A lifetime out on the water had left his skin looking like a three-dimensional roadmap from which a beak nose protruded and into which his sunken lips disappeared.

Without missing a beat, Casey stepped to the side of the lady standing ahead of him in line.

"He doesn't speak French," the woman said before Casey had a chance to speak. Louise had warned Casey that some of *Bretagne*'s older residents spoke only the traditional dialect. It was different enough from French that they wouldn't understand the language unless they had made a real effort to learn it.

"Oh," Casey said to the woman who had volunteered the information, "well, maybe you could help me…"

The woman looked straight ahead and, in perfect French, said, "I don't speak French either."

Not for the first time since her arrival on the Ile de Batz, a tingle of pure furor traveled through Casey's body. Every instinct made her want to lash out physically at the hateful, condescending ruffians who populated the island. How could sensible human beings treat a perfect stranger with such outright animosity? She had done absolutely nothing to earn their scorn, and the injustice of their behavior infuriated her.

Casey took an involuntary step back from the woman who had so coarsely dismissed her. She looked from her face to the face of the gentleman standing in line behind her and failed to read any trace of kindness in their expressions. With a final vestige of hope, she turned her attention to the man sitting behind the desk. He appeared to be in his mid-forties and was somewhat more civilized looking than the other two. He had sold Casey her phone card in a nearly affable manner and stood out as her last chance at finding a chimney sweep.

The post office worker looked up and met Casey's gaze. He knew he was next in line for her question and seemed completely unnerved by the prospect. His eyes darted from Casey to the woman he was serving. What he read there must have packed a healthy threat. With a final, apologetic glance in Casey's direction, he lowered his head over the stamps he was preparing for his customer and didn't look up again.

At a loss, Casey returned to the phone cubicle and sat for a while, her mind blank, the adrenalin of her encounter with the post office patrons flushing her cheeks. She finally reached for the phonebook and located a chimney sweep in Roscoff, the small town from which she'd taken the ferry to the island.

She cleared her throat softly and dialed the number.

"*Allo!*" an energetic voice said as the line picked up on the other end.

"Oh, hello," Casey answered hopefully. "My name is Casey Jensen—I live on the Ile de Batz."

"You're the *américaine*," he stated, leaving Casey to wonder if the entire West coast of France knew of her presence on the island or if her accent was just so bad that people felt the need to acknowledge her origins.

"I've had a bit of a problem with my chimney and wondered if you'd be able to…"

"We don't do the island, *madame*," he interrupted.

"But you're only a few minutes from here."

"Nope. Can't help you."

"Then do you know of someone here who can…"

But the line had gone dead.

Casey listened to the dial tone and her accelerated heartbeat combining in her ear. There was no central heating in the Kermadec house. She had found two small electric radiators—one in the kitchen and one in her bedroom—but she knew they would be of little use once the bitter, damp cold of winter truly set in. The only means she had of eradicating the humidity from her walls and of creating some sort of ambient heat was the fireplace in the living room. Without its warmth, the winter would be unbearable.

Casey suddenly realized that the length of her stay in France was directly connected to her ability to heat the house. Without the fireplace in functional order, she'd be back in Illinois before Christmas.

Gathering her purse, pen and paper, Casey left the post office defeated. She hadn't slept well after the chimney fire, but she couldn't nap—not with jetlag still interrupting her nights. She hadn't eaten all day, but she didn't have the energy to go to the store again. She had seen only a fraction of the island since her arrival, but she didn't have the courage to risk running into more inhospitable islanders.

With a defeated weight in her steps, Casey headed home.

∞

The weeks after Casey's meeting with Pastor Scott marked a change in her state of mind. Having endured the trauma of complete loss of control over her emotions, she endeavored to never let it happen again. The marrow-deep chill of emotional numbness became her salvation. At the first sign of noisy chaos in her mind, she quelled it. When something or someone required an emotional response, she withdrew. If memories came to harass her, she smothered them with sleep or waking oblivion. Survival instincts dictated her emotional death. Only rare, random bursts of anger—brief, irrational, and often unfounded—occasionally ruffled the torpid surface of her emotions.

Layle and Troy had learned not to ask her how she was. They made sure she was fed and Layle even occasionally suggested that Casey take a shower. This certainly wasn't the cohabitation they had envisioned when Casey had called in early September to ask if she could move in with them for a while. It was Layle who had answered the phone.

"Casey? You don't sound like yourself."

Casey had tried to recall her prepared speech. "I think it would be good for me to take you up on your offer," she said, her words misshapen and her voice unsteady.

There was a moment of silence on Layle's end of the line. "You're ready to move in with us?"

Casey pondered the question. Ready? No. Willing? Not really. On the brink of irreparable harm? Probably. Likely. She had raided her medicine cabinet the night before in search of anything that might allow her to be still for just an hour. A *minute* of "absence" was all she needed. Just a moment of nothingness, where images didn't saturate her mind and her own inner voice didn't spew its litany of accusations, regrets, and soul-searing remorse. She needed something drastic to anesthetize her or to distract her. But she knew, in that small portion of her consciousness still capable of rational thought, that anything that truly allowed her to distance herself from the suffocating tumult in her mind would be a permanent and fatal solution.

Although her life had been a waking hell for two weeks, a deeply buried desire to live had prevented her from swallowing the whole inventory of medication she found in her cabinet. She settled for twice the prescribed dosage of nighttime pain pills and cursed when she awoke from a traumatic nightmare eight hours later, just as overwhelmed as she had felt hours before, and just as angry with herself for lacking the strength to exit the turbulence of her mind completely.

She picked up the phone, still groggy from hours of drugged sleep, and opted for distraction—since oblivion hadn't provided any relief.

"I can come over and pick you up right away," Layle said.

"I have to pack…" Casey hedged.

"I can help you."

There was a tug of war going on in Casey's mind. If she took this step, she would lose the solitude that had been her friend and her tormentor, she would become reliant on others, and she would have to answer their questions and put up with their concern. If she stayed in her own home, she risked everything. Not that everything mattered anymore. She'd given up her job. She'd refused her friends' calls. She'd holed up in her private space until it felt like a crypt. She wasn't sure what it was that had made her call her sister and accept her offer to move in with her. All she knew was that natural instincts had been so rare in recent weeks that she had to trust them when they manifested themselves.

Layle had come over in her minivan to help Casey to pack and, with just two suitcases, they had driven the short distance to the home Layle shared with her husband and two kids. The guest-room was a large space, comfortably furnished and tastefully decorated, but Casey noticed neither. She told her sister that she needed rest, curled up on the bed, and fell instantly asleep. Layle unpacked her suitcases as she slept.

Casey's meeting with Pastor Scott had changed Layle too. She stopped asking so many questions and became content just to have Casey with her. She watched her sister like a hawk, hoping for any sign of improvement, but she never commented on her state of mind, on the pallor of her skin, on the days on end she spent indoors, or on the disappointment of two children who had been so excited to have Auntie Casey living under their roof. Instead, Layle became the steady caregiver who met Casey's needs before she realized she had them and gave her the space and solitude she craved. There was never any doubt in Casey's mind about her sister's love and concern, but she was grateful Layle hadn't pushed for more therapy since the day Pastor Scott had sent her hurtling head-first into the numb apathy that now spared her from the raw ache of reality.

# *Chapter Seven*

"Hey, did you really have a chimney fire last night?" Pierrot's excited voice brought Casey out of her reverie. She'd been sitting on the top step outside her home since her visit to the post office, not quite ready to go inside and face the desolate, damp house.

Pierrot stood at the gate looking up at her with excitement on his face.

"Come on up!" she called to him, surprisingly grateful for the distraction. She hadn't welcomed company in so long that her positive response to Pierrot's appearance took her by surprise.

He catapulted through the gate, walking on legs that seemed too long and uncoordinated. He reminded Casey of a young Bambi, ungainly and utterly irresistible.

"So did you?" he asked when he had reached Casey's front steps. He stood there, one foot on the bottom step and both arms crossed on the end of the metallic railing. He looked at her eagerly, clearly hoping for a dramatic retelling of the story.

Casey frowned in confusion. "How did you hear about it?" she asked, amazed again at the rate news traveled on the island.

"Luke," he answered. He leaned toward her. "Did it smoke up your house? Did you have to call the firemen?"

"Are there actually firemen on the island?" Casey asked, surprised.

"Yeah—and a fire truck too. Cédric keeps it at his farm

but it doesn't look very good because the seagulls use it for a perch. So did you call him? Did he drive out here?"

Casey started to laugh—then stopped herself. It felt somehow obscene for her to be laughing when so much had gone wrong and was still going wrong. "I wouldn't have known how to call him if I had *wanted* to," she said. "But Luke put the fire out without the firemen's help."

"Did he throw water on it?" Pierrot's fascination with the details of Casey's story and the enthusiasm of his questions was refreshing.

"Actually, he found some kind of flare and put it in the fireplace," she told Pierrot, still unsure of what the flare was and what it had done. "And then he hosed down the roof around the chimney to make sure it didn't catch fire." Talking with Pierrot brought back memories of being a teacher, and she was surprised by the wistfulness the memories evoked.

"He is *so* cool!" Pierrot exclaimed, slapping his leg with glee. It was obvious the boy worshiped the ground his elder walked on.

"Do you know what that flare is?" Casey asked, finally voicing the question she'd had since the night before.

"Oh sure. It's made for chimney fires. There's a chemical in it that goes up the chimney and sucks the oxygen out of the air so whatever is on fire up there can't burn anymore. Everybody has them."

"Oh," Casey said. She hadn't expected such a thorough answer from the boy. She assumed he hadn't received much of an education. He used elementary vocabulary when he wasn't talking about chimney flares, and he seemed to spend way too much time loitering in the streets during school hours. But he knew enough to explain the chemical process of the fire extinguisher to her. She wondered what he did when he wasn't sitting by the harbor waiting to assist incoming fishermen.

"So why did you call Luke instead of Cédric?" Pierrot asked. "He doesn't have a truck." The boy was clearly enamored with the islands fire-truck-slash-seagull-perch.

Casey shivered as she recalled the outrageous coincidence that had brought Luke to her house just in time to save it.

"I actually didn't call him," she answered Pierrot's question. She frowned. "All I know is that he saw the fire and somehow just turned up."

"He is *so* cool!"

"So you've said."

"I know," Pierrot enthused, "but he really is cool!"

Based on the fact that the house behind her was still standing, Casey had to agree.

The church clock rang five times and Pierrot looked around in surprise.

"Was that five?" he asked.

Casey glanced at her watch. "It's two minutes past."

"I've got to run. There's a ferry coming in soon."

He turned to hurry down the path toward the gate.

"Pierrot?" Casey called after him.

"*Oui, madame?*"

"Do you know of any chimney sweeps on the island?"

He took an eager step in her direction and smiled. "I could do it for you if you'd like."

Casey was sure the job would be done with verve, but given her recent problems, she figured employing a professional would be wise.

"It should probably be done by a professional," she said kindly and, seeing his face sadden, added, "Just because of the fire last night. I need to make sure there's no structural damage."

Pierrot seemed comforted by her explanation. "There's Cédric," he said, answering her question. "But I don't think he'd do it." He turned to leave, shoving his hands deep into his pockets.

"Wait!" Casey called after him, standing up and moving closer to the railing. "Why wouldn't he help me?" Curiosity and annoyance wrestled in her mind.

Pierrot shrugged. "Because you're *l'américaine*," he answered, as if it was an obvious explanation. He turned and trotted out the gate, retracing his steps a moment later to latch it behind him. Then, with a parting wave, he galloped down the street toward the docks.

Casey watched the boys run down the soccer field and marveled at their speed and precision. Though she'd attended plenty of Glen Ellyn High's games, it still impressed her to see young men who seemed completely purposeless in their academic careers become such single-minded warriors on the field. Marilyn sat beside her, as she did at every game, balancing Casey's slightly less enthusiastic spectating with her boisterous cheering and brash referee-bashing. For a conservative, usually sedate woman, she put on quite a show at these sporting events. Casey had begun to notice that some of the spectators sitting around them were regulars, and she wondered whether they came for the game or for Marilyn's sideshow. The score was 3-2 for Glen Ellyn High, and the tension in the stands was palpable. With just under five minutes to go, every time the ball rolled near the goals the final outcome of the game was in jeopardy.

"Gooooooooooooo, Tigers!" Marilyn screamed, brandishing a hand-painted sign above her head. When the referee made a questionable call, she was the first on her feet yelling, "No way, Ref! No way!!" then advising the guys to ignore the "jailbird ref" and focus on the ball. There were smiles in the stands, but Marilyn wasn't aware of them. Her attention was completely wrapped up in "her boys" on the field.

Casey watched Ben, impressed by his dexterous ball handling and his leadership as team captain. Other players, some with longer histories at the school than his, listened attentively when he yelled instructions at them or decided what plays to execute. The coach seemed to trust him implicitly, sometimes allowing Ben to take over at half time. That an eighteen-year old was capable of analyzing a game he was participating in and of using that analysis to motivate and organize his teammates was astounding. Yet he did it with seeming ease and understatement. His athletic merit was obvious even to Casey's untrained eye, and she understood why colleges had been calling to recruit this promising player.

There were ten seconds left on the clock and Marilyn was leading the crowd in the countdown. On the field, the battle continued fiercely.

"Five! Four! Three! Two! One!" And Marilyn shrieked like a Banshee, waving her sign victoriously above her head. Casey laughed at her exuberant hug and clapped with the rest of the crowd as the players shook hands and trotted off the field toward the bench.

"Come on! We're going down there," Marilyn announced, grabbing Casey's sleeve and pulling her behind her down the crowded stairs.

"Wait!" Casey said, laughing at she wove her way around spectators clogging the stairway. "We really shouldn't go down there, Marilyn! The last thing they want to see is two teachers!"

"Correction," Marilyn said over her shoulder, still plowing her way through the parents, students, and staff members who had attended the game. "That's one teacher and one world-class fan. They'll be happy to see me. You? They'll just put up with you!"

"Hey!" Casey exclaimed, feigning hurt feelings.

"Oh, shut up and keep walking," Marilyn instructed, laughing and out of breath.

By the time they reached the players' bench, some of the athletes, caked in mud and dripping with sweat, had collected their things and were heading to the showers. Marilyn intercepted a couple of them and gave them strong enough smacks on the back to make them stagger. She raved about their playing and ranted about the arbitrating, submitting them to a condensed version of what the spectators in the stands had heard for nearly two hours.

Casey saw Ben among the players heading to the locker room. His eyes were downcast and he rolled his shoulder painfully, slightly injured by one of the miracle saves he'd made during the last seconds of the game. As he passed within a few feet of her, Casey called his name. When he turned in her direction, she mouthed, "Great game" to him. It was very much the Team Captain who walked over to her and thanked her formally for attending the game. Casey found his gratitude endearing and complimented him on his playing.

"You were amazing out there," she said.

He shrugged.

Casey looked around at the parents congratulating their sons and asked, "Are your parents here? They've got to be so proud of you!"

He looked directly at her, his long blond hair, unusually tousled, lending him a boyish air. "They've never come," he said so quietly that Casey wondered if she'd heard him correctly.

But Ben was walking away already, still rolling his shoulder and thanking spectators for attending the game.

Casey was standing there when Marilyn materialized beside her and grabbed her arm.

"This calls for beer," she said loudly enough to attract more stares.

"I don't like beer, Marilyn."

"Well then, you can have a glass of milk!"

"It's a piña colada or nothing at all, my friend," Casey informed her.

"That' a girl!" came Marilyn's immediate reply. With a smack on Casey's back that knocked the breath from her, the two friends set off toward the parking lot.

Casey was surprised, on the following Monday morning, when Marilyn delivered another of Ben's journal entries to her in the staff lounge. Marilyn wiggled an eyebrow as she passed it to Casey then left the room.

Not knowing what to expect, Casey unfolded the paper gingerly. It was dated four months prior and addressed to his parents. The fact that she held the original in her hand suggested that he had never sent it.

*Dear mom and dad,*

*It strikes me as pretty freakin' warped that you called a family meeting tonight to let us know that we need to spend more time with you. Pretty amazingly, freakin' rich. Rachel and Ian played the part of the dutiful little children really well, don't you think? They looked all worried and sorry and promised to spend less time with their friends and less time doing what they love and blah blah blah. And you sat there and thanked them for being so respectful and so honest and so considerate. And I sat there wondering when it was going to be YOUR turn to be respectful and honest and considerate.*

*And then you looked at me with this "So are you going to promise too?" expression—like if my kid brother and my kid sister can do it I should be able to do it too. Please. You really don't know me at all, do you.*

*Maybe that's your own freakin' fault, by the way. Ever think of that? Maybe if you had spent one percent of the time on me that you spent on total strangers, I'd be more than another soccer uniform to buy and another plane ticket to save for. And FYI, it was YOUR idea to fly all over the world. I never asked for any of it. But you were so CALLED to do it that you didn't even bother to ask any of us.*

*So now you want us to BOND and become a REAL*

*family. Too freakin' late, guys! We were all cooped up in a tiny apartment in Tajikistan for—what?—five YEARS and you were barely home enough to notice we were outgrowing our shoes. You can't blame that on us. We were there. Well, three of us were there. You packed Angela and Susan off pretty fast once you figured out they were going to cramp your style and demand some of your precious time.*

*So yeah. That's what I wanted to say. Oh, and by the way, there's a soccer game next weekend. But don't let that interfere with your visiting and counseling and evangelizing and obeying and repenting and flogging yourselves and crap. (I know you don't flog yourselves—that was a bit of humor, not that you'd recognize it if it bit you in the ass.) So anyway, yeah. Soccer game. There's a scout coming from U of I to check me out. I guess he thinks I'm pretty good. How 'bout you guys? Do you think I'm good? Oh, wait! That's right! You wouldn't know. You've never been to a single game. It wouldn't be so hard to take if your names weren't on my birth certificate.*

*Hey, here's to a few more souls saved today! Maybe we can sit around and BOND over that later on.*

*Outta here.*

*B.*

Casey slowly folded the paper and tucked it into the outside pocket of her bag. She felt drained from the reading and wondered how it felt to be *inside* that mind. The frustration and sheer weariness... Casey wondered if there was anything she could do to change Ben's circumstances, but no solution seemed viable. She could speak with his parents, but they probably wouldn't be very receptive—not if Ben's journal entry was accurate. She could report them to social services, but their children were well cared for in a practical sense, and who would blame the parents for allowing their kids to see the world while they worked for a religious organization?

At a loss, Casey rose and went to the window. She had always found comfort in watching the students interact when they didn't know they were being observed. But there was no comfort in that today. She only wondered, as she watched, how many of them hid secrets like Ben's that they didn't dare express.

*Another day*, Casey mused as she lay in bed. She had heard the morning's first birds and seen the sky brighten, though a depressing gray fog still hung over the island. This was the coldest morning yet, and though she had hopped out of bed briefly to turn on the electric radiator, she had quickly crawled back under the feather comforter she'd found in the hallway closet.

And there she'd lain, for over two hours, pondering her circumstances and trying to ignore the pungent smell coming from the small radiator. She was grateful for its warmth—it seemed to draw some of the moisture out of the air. But she still wished there were another means of heating the house. She suspected that what little heat had accumulated in her bedroom would dissipate the moment she opened the door. This was no way to spend a winter.

Another thought brought her musing to a standstill.

The porcelain commode in the downstairs bathroom was unpleasant enough in this fall weather, but minus a seat, it would be downright unbearable in the winter. She needed to do something about that—and do it fast. But that probably required a trip to Roscoff and, much as her toilet woes bothered her, the prospect of a half-day excursion seemed an insurmountable obstacle.

Casey was pondering alternatives when she heard a knock on the door.

Grabbing her robe off the foot of the bed, she hurried downstairs. With no peephole in her front door, all she could do was open it and hope for the best.

An unhappy looking man who appeared to be in his thirties stood there. He was dressed in black pants and a double-breasted short black jacket. He wore a wide black belt over the jacket, its shiny metallic buckle a perfect match to two vertical rows of polished buttons. There was a red scarf tied at the man's neck, and a ratty black high top perched on a head of blonde hair that looked like hay escaping from a loose bale. A coiled, stiff cable hung on his shoulder. He was the epitome of the traditional French chimney sweep Casey had read about in history books. If she had been in the States, she would have assumed this was a practical joke. But she was on the Ile de Batz where surprises seemed to be a way of life.

"Can I help you?" she asked, drawing her robe closer against the damp morning air.

"You had a problem with your fireplace?" he asked. His accent was thick and nearly unintelligible.

"Yes, I…"

But he had already brushed past her and entered her living room, dropping the coiled cable from his shoulder and kneeling to look up the chimney.

"I need newspaper," he said gruffly.

Casey, standing stunned in the doorway to the living room, told him she didn't have any.

The man grunted a response and pulled a newspaper from his bag. He spread the pages on the floor around the fireplace, and shoved the length of cable upward into the chimney. There was a circular, metallic star at the end of the cable with sharp, stiff points which she assumed would scrape the tar from the inside of the chimney. Debris began to fall rapidly and bounce across the floor, fine soot darkening the air and settling in a black layer on the furniture and the floor.

Unwilling to watch any more, Casey went to close the front door then just stood there, in the hallway, waiting for the sound of scraping and the occasional coughing coming from the living room to stop.

Minutes later, the chimney sweep's blackened form came out of the living room leaving sooty footprints on the floor and brushed past Casey. He opened the front door and left the house. When she didn't see him heading for the gate, Casey stepped outside the door and found the chimney sweep retrieving a ladder he must have left leaning against the wall when he arrived. He walked around the house with it. There was a metallic clatter as he raised the ladder, then the sound of heavy footsteps on the rungs as he climbed to the roof of the house. Casey heard more debris falling into the living room and hurried in to assess the damage.

There was soot everywhere. It blanketed the fireplace and the bricks surrounding it, extending thickly at least three feet in all directions. The filth in the air was still settling and Casey knew the mess would take hours to clean completely.

She heard the chimney sweep's descending steps on the ladder outside and headed to the door with her wallet in hand, ready to thank him profusely despite the damage done to her living room. But the man walked down the path to the gate and off down the street even after Casey called to him to wait.

He was passing the low wall by the church when Casey saw Luke get up and move to his side. He handed over a few bills and patted the chimney sweep's shoulder. It was a friendly gesture. The chimney sweep continued on his way and Luke paused for a moment, looking in Casey's direction, then disappeared in the same direction the chimney sweep had gone.

Standing at her front door in her robe, a living room covered in soot behind her, Casey didn't know whether to cry with relief or rage in frustration. Since crying hadn't been high on her agenda for the past few months, she opted to take out her frustration on the living room instead.

∞

Ben threw down his pen and stormed out of the classroom. The startled students looked at each other uncomprehendingly. They'd been quietly concentrating on their French exam before Ben's exit. Casey followed him out into the corridor but didn't see him anywhere. She walked around the corner to Marilyn's office.

"Have you seen Ben Landon?" she asked.

Marilyn had been staring out the front door when Casey approached her desk. She raised an eyebrow and nodded her head toward the school entrance. "Out there," she said. "And he didn't look happy."

"Could you watch my class for a minute? They're just taking a test..."

"No worries," Marilyn said, levering herself out of her chair. "Anna, will you get the phones?" she asked the secretary sitting at the desk on the other side of the office. Anna waved her away.

"I won't be long," Casey assured her friend as she rounded the corner.

She faced the front doors of the school and braced herself. Confronting unruly students was never a pleasant task. But when that student was someone like Ben Landon, it became unpleasant *and* complex.

He was sitting on the stone construction in the middle of the circle of grass that fronted the high school. He sat on the short pillar just to the left of the "Glen Ellyn High School" sign that proclaimed the year of the school's founding in weathered gold letters. As Casey approached, she could see that he was speaking out loud to himself and that his body was rigid with anger. She came up behind him, clearing her throat lightly to let him know she was there. She stopped behind the chest-high wall with her arms crossed on top of it.

"Want to tell me what happened back there?"

"No."

"Was it something about the test?"

"No."

Casey didn't know how to proceed. She was conscious of the eyes of dozens of students watching through their classroom windows. She found an indentation in the wall and used it as a foothold to climb up onto it, a foot or two away from her student, facing the other direction. She didn't see the turn-of-the-century building in front of her, though. Her mind was on the young man at her side from whom tension emanated like a palpable electric field. She couldn't leave him alone in the state he was in.

"Did something happen at school today that…"

"No."

"Did something happen at home?"

Silence. And then, "I'm not talking about it."

"Well," Casey said quietly, "you might not be using words to talk about it, but your exit from the classrooms spoke pretty clearly."

She heard cutting sarcasm in his voice when he said, "I didn't mean to disturb your precious class."

She turned her head to look at him. "The class will get over it. It's you I'm concerned about."

A short, bitter laugh escaped him before she had even finished her sentence.

"You find it humorous that I'm concerned about you?" she asked.

His shoulders slumped a bit, losing some of their previous rigidity.

"Tell me what happened."

Casey let the silence lengthen. She drew comfort from the fact that he hadn't left school grounds. If he had truly wanted to be left alone, he would have disappeared altogether. They sat in tense silence for several minutes. Casey used the time to collect her thoughts and calm her nerves. Ben sat immobile, staring down. He took a deep breath and Casey could hear him holding it until he let it out in a rush. Still, she didn't push.

A chapter from *The Little Prince* came to her mind as she waited for Ben to drum up the courage to communicate. In the story, the Prince met a fox that he found to be beautiful and fascinating. The Prince explained to the fox that he was looking for friends and the fox answered that they couldn't be friends because he hadn't been tamed. When the Prince asked about the meaning of the word "tamed", the fox explained, "One only understands the things that one tames." And later he pleaded with the boy, "If you want a friend, tame me."

Casey had read the book a hundred times and taught it so often that she could quote entire pages verbatim. The story had always fascinated her because of the depth of its symbolism and the accuracy of its depiction of human relationships. Now, as she sat next to this young man who had apparently never been tamed—by anyone—she remembered the fox's instructions to the boy, marveling that it was the fox in the story who was begging to be tamed, not the boy begging to tame the fox.

When the Prince asked the fox what taming him required, the fox answered simply that the boy needed to turn up every day and sit. At first, he would sit a fair distance away, and every day he would move a little closer. He was not to speak. He just needed to be there.

And so Casey sat, the minutes ticking by, waiting for Ben to speak *if* he so desired, content that he wasn't running.

"My parents are moving back to Tajikistan."

Casey couldn't control her shocked intake of air. She hoped she had heard him wrong. A riot of emotions—anger, frustration, disbelief, contempt, grief—slammed into her mind and robbed her of speech. Neither she nor Ben said anything for a few moments longer.

When Casey had sifted through her thoughts, in a carefully controlled voice, she asked, "When did you find out?"

Pause. "This morning."

"When do they leave?"

"In August."

She felt anger constricting her lungs. If she, a teacher who had known Ben only a few weeks, could see what their departure was doing to him, how could his own parents, in good conscience, abandon a child so desperately in need of security? She seethed at the injustice and fought for calm.

"Tell me what's going on in your head," she said.

She didn't fear his silences anymore. She knew they were the precursors of deliberate words.

"Let them go," he finally said.

"You don't mean that…"

"I mean it," he corrected her before she had finished her thought. "Let them go the hell back to *saving souls*!"

The last words were spoken with such venom that Casey felt her breath catch and tears flood her eyes.

"Ben…"

But he had opened the floodgates of his agony and anger, and there was no stopping the torrent of bitter, scathing, honest feelings. With every evangelical word, his lips twisted in a sneer and his voice slithered into a sickly, evil sound. It was a litany of blame, a virulent condemnation of all he despised. "Let them bring the *Gospel* to the lost *souls* at the *ends of the earth*! Let them love the *sinner* and hate the *sin*! Let them screw over their own *family* to save a bunch of *strangers*! Let them *dedicate* and *commit* their freakin' *lives* to reaching the *unreached* for the Lord—*Jesus—Christ!*"

His final three words had been uttered with such ferociousness that he fell forward off the low wall and dropped to the ground on his knees, breaking into a harsh, guttural laugh that sent shivers down Casey's spine. She climbed off the wall and came around to his side, hurriedly putting a hand on his shoulder to make sure he was alright.

"Don't *touch* me!" he screamed, throwing her hand off and staggering to his feet, his eyes wild and wet, his face flushed, his body shaking. "Get your freakin' Christian hands *off me!*"

As shocked as she was, Casey couldn't let him go.

"Talk to your parents, Ben," she pleaded. "Let them know how you feel."

"Let them know how I *feel?*" he shrieked. He spread his arms wide and turned to face the school where students were clustered at the windows. "They don't freakin' know I'm *alive!*"

Casey saw him gag, the bile of his emotions becoming a physical retch. He swallowed hard and clasped his arms across his middle.

"Ben," she said, reaching toward him again.

He came erect then, his eyes burning Casey with their acid, staring straight at her, straight through her, his face contorted in a violent sneer, his arms now held rigidly at his sides.

"You—all—repulse—me!" he spit out, each word more hateful than the last. Then with an obscene gesture aimed at the students observing from their classrooms, he ran—staggering at first, then faster and faster—with a haunted, broken, liberating scream.

## Chapter Eight

"Hey, I hear you got your chimney problem fixed!"

Pierrot's voice made Casey stop in mid-stride and turn to greet him. He sauntered up to her and noticed the *baguette* protruding from her canvas bag.

"Been to Marthe's, huh?"

Casey frowned. "Is she the baker?"

"Her husband's the baker. She just sells the bread," Pierrot explained. "But yeah, that's her."

Casey had finally figured out, on her third trip to the bakery, that Marthe was going out to the kitchen to get the bread she gave Casey rather than taking it from the large upright baskets lining the wall behind the counter.

When Casey pointed at the bread display and asked for one of those *baguettes*, Marthe shook her head and pushed the one she'd brought from the kitchen toward Casey.

"This bread is…" Casey struggled to remember the world for 'stale' in French, and settled instead for 'old'. "This bread is old," she said.

"*Mais non!*" Marthe said, gesturing for Casey to take the *baguette* she offered and be done with it.

But Casey had had enough of eating stale bread. With no preservatives in it, French bread began to harden in hours, and the loaf she was buying now would be rock hard by breakfast. It was already harder than it ought to be.

"I'd like one of *those*, please," Casey repeated, a stubborn tilt to her chin.

An elderly woman at the back of the line grumbled something in the Breton dialect, clearly impatient with the hold-up. Marthe reached for a loaf of fresh bread and fairly flung it at Casey.

"Here," she said harshly.

Casey smiled as sweetly as her acting skills would allow and handed the woman her coins. "*Bonne soirée!*" she called lightly as she left the *boulangerie*. Not surprisingly, no one wished her a good evening in return.

Running into Pierrot on her way home had significantly lifted her spirits.

"So did he do a good job?" the quirky young man asked.

"Who?"

"Cédric. He did your chimney right?"

"Oh, right. Yes. He certainly pulled a lot of—stuff—out of it!"

"Good," the young man said. "I told Luke that you were having trouble finding someone to clean it, and he said he'd take care of it."

"So *that's* how he found out," Casey said.

"Yeah," Pierrot answered, a faint blush coloring his cheeks. "I figured maybe it would help."

"I'll think of you every time I light a fire," Casey laughed. She was gratified to see Pierrot stand a little taller with pride. "Now if you can find me a toilet seat and a blow-dryer, I'll be indebted to you forever!"

Pierrot looked nervous. "Oh, I don't know if I…"

"It's okay," she hurried to add, touching his arm lightly. "I was just joking. I'll get over to Roscoff eventually and find what I need there."

"Okay…" With the conversation waning, Pierrot started to get fidgety. "Uhm, I guess I'll see you around then," he said.

"Sure. I'll see you around, Pierrot."

Casey had just walked a few steps when she called back to him.

He turned with a loud "*Ouai??*" that reverberated in the near empty streets.

Casey stepped toward him to avoid disturbing the quiet any further. "I'd like to thank Luke," she said. "Do you know where I can find him?"

"Sure! He's always at *Le Bigorneau* in the evenings."

"Oh. Okay. Well… Maybe I'll drop in there sometime and say thank you." She had no intention of entering the restaurant again. One afternoon with Marguerite had been more than enough.

"Hey, I'm going there now! It's my turn to work the bar tonight," he said proudly. "I'll walk with you!"

"No, I…"

"And then I can serve you a beer." He blushed. "Or coffee. Or something."

Casey was torn between the sheer terror of a repeat-visit to Marguerite's lair and the eagerness of the young man who was her only friend on the island. Fear finally gave in to kindness as she reluctantly let Pierrot walk her to the restaurant.

The air was thick with smoke when they entered, and the sound of voices, music, and kitchen activity were just as thick. But as soon as one patron recognized her through the smog, a deathly quiet she had come to recognize settled over *Le Bigorneau*.

Unaware of the underlying tension, Pierrot trotted up to the bar with a loud, "*Eh, Luke!* Look who's here!"

All the eyes that had been looking at anything *but* Casey suddenly converged on Luke.

He was sitting at the end of the bar with a sheaf of papers and a calculator in front of him. He'd been in the process of typing in numbers with the eraser end of his pencil when Pierrot had interrupted his work. He looked from his calculator to Pierrot, then slid his glance across the room to Casey.

Casey was sure she had never experienced a more unsettling moment in her life. She realized that her small victory in

Marthe's shop had inflated her confidence beyond her capacities and that she had entered a situation she was incapable of managing. When Luke looked at her, every other eye in the restaurant did too—as if his making eye contact with her gave them permission to do so as well. Casey was only vaguely aware of the physical context: the heat, the smells of food and drink, the dozen or so men and women scattered around the room. What was overwhelmingly clear was a familiar static in her mind, a crescendoing chaos that threatened to engulf her. She had taken such care in recent weeks to protect herself from threatening circumstances, yet had somehow failed to foresee this one. She felt completely exposed, utterly despised, and unbearably alone. Her mental equilibrium teetered. Her face blanched and her palms became moist. Everything around her seemed to shrink away, taking her ability to breathe with it. Though this moment had nothing to do with the summer's events, it had unleashed its demons and lent them relentless power.

She wanted to leave, but couldn't move her legs. She wanted to apologize for intruding on the patrons' space, but she couldn't formulate a sound. She wanted to scream at Pierrot for forcing her into taking such a reckless risk, but she couldn't muster the energy to be angry.

Casey was so focused on trying to control the growing tumult in her head that she didn't notice Luke pushing away from the bar and walking toward her. She started visibly when he touched her arm and peered more closely into her face. "*Ça va?*" she heard him ask. All she could do was shake her head, willing him to put an end to the anxiety and powerlessness that were suffocating her.

"Pierrot, take over at the bar," she heard him say.

She felt his hand at her elbow turning her around and guiding her out the door. The cold evening air hit her like a physical blow, and she inhaled a deep, painful lungful of oxygen. Her stomach was churning and a wave of dizziness made her reach out and grab Luke's sleeve to stay upright.

He steadied her while she took several more deep breaths of ocean air.

"*Ça va passer*," she heard him say, and his promise that it would pass somehow allowed her to relax a little more. She focused on the pattern in his slate-grey sweater while she commanded herself to relax, to breathe more deeply, to let the chaos recede.

When she finally came to her senses, she realized that she was still standing with Luke, one of his hands on her arm, steadying her, and her eyes still fixed on the front of his sweater.

"*Ça va?*" he asked again.

"*Ça va*," she replied, hoping she wasn't lying about feeling better. Though the tumult had subsided, she always feared that it would return immediately if she wasn't vigilant.

"*Venez*," he said, escorting her across the street to the low stone wall that bordered the harbor. "Sit here."

"Thank you," she said, then realized that this humiliation had been caused by her desire to say just that.

"They'll warm up to you in time," he said.

She looked at him in confusion.

"The islanders," he explained. "They'll come around."

She laughed then, because his statement was ridiculous.

"They will *never* warm up to me," she said as fiercely as her voice allowed. Then, with sarcasm, added, "I'm *l'américaine*."

Pierrot popped his head out the door. "You want your coat?" he asked.

"I won't be long," Luke answered, still standing next to Casey, his hands in his pockets now.

"Okay," Pierrot said, ducking back inside.

"He works for you?" Casey asked.

"He does odd jobs."

She took a few more deep breaths and was relieved to feel her muscles unclenching.

"You do this often?" he asked, but there was no mockery

in his voice. His question seemed sincere.

"What?" she asked, an ironic smile barely lifting the corners of her mouth, "Walk into enemy territory and freak out in front of my worst critics? No. Not really."

"This isn't enemy territory," he said quietly, lowering himself to sit beside her on the wall.

Casey's laugh was harsher than she intended. "Those people would lynch me if they had the chance," she said, not in the least exaggerating her convictions.

"Those people wouldn't hurt a stray dog," he said.

"But a stray American…" She let the sentence hang.

He didn't answer for a moment. When he finally did, his voice spoke his loyalty to the people of the Ile de Batz. "Their distaste of Americans—and most foreigners—is ancestral. They've been invaded too many times to welcome anyone with open arms."

"No kidding."

He acknowledged her sarcasm with a half-smile. "But their acceptance of a person is unconditional once they grant it," he continued. "Give them time to get over their traditional misgivings and if they grow to like you, you'll have their loyalty for life."

Casey was opening her mouth to point out the injustice of that approach when a sudden realization froze her in mid-thought.

"You…" She was aghast. "You…"

He smiled and, in his enigmatic way, said, "Maybe you should take another breath."

"You said that in English," she finally blurted, angry at him for reasons she didn't understand. "You speak *English*," she repeated, staring at him as if his face would explain the mystery.

"I'm getting cold," he said, rising to his feet.

"And it's *perfect* English," she added.

"I'm heading back inside. You're welcome to come in for a cup of coffee, if you'd like. It's on the house."

Horror temporarily superceded her shock at his linguistic skills. "Are you kidding?" she asked, incredulity tightening her voice, her eyes widening with panic. "I'm not going back in there. I *can't* go back in there." Now that she could speak to him in English, she found the words coming faster than they had in days. "You don't know what it's like. Those people hate me," she said with more passion than she intended, her throat constricting with long-building emotions. She would not let them out. She would not let this stranger see her weakness. She stood and located her bag, slinging it over her shoulder and shaking her head at this man who had rescued her more often than she cared to admit. "I can't do it. Really."

"That's okay," he said. Though his voice was expressionless, his eyes confirmed his words. He wasn't judging her.

She took a few steps in the direction of her house then turned back, speaking just as his hand reached for the door of the restaurant.

"I..." She was at a loss. "Are you American?" she finally asked, hope softening her gaze.

He smiled then—as if a private memory was passing through his mind. Even in the darkness and with the distance between them, she was startled by the brightness of his eyes and the intensity of his gaze. "Come in and have coffee sometime," he said. "I'll answer your questions."

"I..."

He was gone before a hasty refusal left her lips.

Her questions would have to wait—and they would wait a long time if getting answers required that she enter *Le Bigorneau* again.

As Casey walked home, she relived the events of the evening. By the time she reached her front door, she had realized that her greatest accomplishment hadn't been finding the courage to wrest fresh bread from Marthe or discovering that Luke spoke English as well as she did. Looking back, she realized that the greater triumph had been in riding out her emotional upheaval without letting it get complete control over her. She had feared for weeks that the next breakdown would utterly consume her, and she had lived in dread of the next time circumstances would push her to the brink. But she had stood in the restaurant with the mental darkness closing in around her, she had felt the quickening of her senses and been aware of the spiraling vortex swirling in to claim her... And it hadn't. Of course, it had taken Luke's assistance, but once he had taken her outside, the cold air and his presence had stifled her demons.

For the first time in what seemed an eternity, Casey didn't feel quite as helpless against her inner foes. They hadn't overwhelmed her tonight. She might be able to fight them off again. The realization gave her an inkling of hope—and slammed her with a paralyzing fear of failure.

Casey felt an uncomfortable disquiet as she approached the door, though the dried flowers hanging just below its high windows seemed welcoming enough. The nametag above the doorbell read "Landon". She pressed the button and heard the bell chime inside the house.

When the door opened, Janet Landon greeted her politely and invited her in. A small, immaculately groomed woman with a pinkish complexion and graying brown hair, she looked like a sensitive, gentle person. "Benjamin is at soccer practice right now, as I told you on the phone," she said. "But he probably won't be long."

Casey looked around the immaculate interior of the Landon home and took in the details. A carpeted staircase that started right next to the front door headed upstairs. Casey could see a formal dining room area through a doorway at the bottom of the stairs, but there appeared to be no tables or chairs in it. Just off the entryway, a sparsely furnished living room boasted of what Casey assumed were Tajik rugs—brightly colored and obviously hand-woven. A large, beige, L-shaped couch covered two walls and framed the old-fashioned packing trunk that served as a coffee table. On each end of the couch, small wooden crates turned on their sides served as end tables and bookshelves. A dresser in desperate need of refinishing sat against another wall with a gallery of family pictures above it.

The kitchen was just off the living room. Casey could see a low fire lit under a large pot on the stove. There was a round table in the breakfast nook surrounded by four chairs. Not five. There were few, if any, decorations in the rooms Casey could see, though the occasional basket or dried-flower arrangement provided minor decorative touches. It was a house that looked lived-in, but not enjoyed.

Casey smiled at Janet Landon. "I'm really here to see you, not Ben," she said, just as she had said on the phone minutes earlier.

"Oh," Janet replied. "Well," she motioned toward the couch, "why don't you have a seat and I'll tear Steve away from his computer." She left the living room and climbed the stairs to the first floor.

Rather than sitting, Casey walked over to the dresser and took a closer look at the family pictures hung unevenly on the wall above it. They were formally posed, framed in different woods, and arranged in chronological order. Casey leaned forward and found the most recent portrait. The family had dressed in denim for the picture, with a few splashes of red, yellow and green accessorizing the jeans. The two youngest children seemed happy enough, their heads tilted a little as they smiled into the camera and their bodies obviously not quite still when the picture was snapped. Ben looked directly into the camera with a gaze that sent shivers down Casey's spine. It was unfocussed and vague. He didn't smile, but stood with stiff arms looking for all the world like a boy facing an execution squad, hoping it would be over soon, but not really caring about his fate. The two older daughters stood next to him, and, though Steve Landon had his arm around one of them, the gesture looked forced and unnatural. The girls were beautiful—both had Ben's thick blond hair and his all-American features—but though they smiled for the picture, there wasn't anything warm in their eyes. Steve looked like a proud father watching over his brood, albeit stiffly, and Janet looked like a calm, dutiful wife and mother.

Casey moved down the row to some of the earlier pictures and found them all posed just as formally. Though the family members were positioned in a close formation, she couldn't help but feel a greater distance between them than their physical nearness suggested. It wasn't until Casey reached the pictures that preceded the Landon's departure for Tajikistan that she noticed a slight difference in the family's dynamics. Although they were still awkwardly posed, the children seemed less stiff. The little ones had goofy smiles on their faces, and even Ben looked to be merely feigning his dislike for the picture-taking process. There still appeared to be an emotional chasm between the parents and their children, but the kids' expressions—especially the older girls'—were more honest and less guarded.

Casey heard soft voices upstairs and moved to sit at one end of the sofa. She stood when Steve Landon walked in followed by his wife and shook his hand. He was a tall, lanky man. His bifocals and beige sweater-vest made him look much older than his years.

"Miss Jensen," he said. "This is a surprise."

"It's nice to see you, Mr. Landon."

Casey took a seat and the Landons followed suit, installing themselves to the left of Casey, just on the other side of the bend in the couch. It left several feet of space between them, but made interaction a bit easier.

"This is about Ben," Steve said.

Casey nodded. "I'm not sure if I'm overstepping my bounds by coming here. Please forgive me if I am."

"Not at all," Janet said sincerely. "If it involves our son, we want to know."

Casey opted not to focus on the gross misstatement.

"Did you notice anything…different about Ben on Monday evening?"

The Landons looked at each other.

Janet seemed concerned when she asked, "Should we have?"

Casey tried to put some order in her thoughts, though she'd been over this conversation in her mind many times since Ben's implosion on Monday.

"Ben had a rough day on Monday," she said, settling for an understatement to let the Landons adjust to the situation. "He left my classroom in the middle of a test and didn't return to school for the two remaining periods of the day."

Although Marilyn had wanted to inform the principal immediately and have him call Ben's parents, Casey had asked if she could meet with them herself to discuss Ben's behavior. The journal entry she had found on her desk the next day had confirmed that a one-on-one conversation was in order.

"He skipped school?" There was obvious displeasure in Steve Landon's low voice.

"Why didn't the school call us?" Janet asked.

"They were going to," Casey explained, "but Ben and I have been having some conversations lately, and I thought it might be better if I spoke with you myself."

Janet looked instantly concerned. "Is he alright?"

Steve shifted uncomfortably on the couch. "He's fine."

"Actually," Casey interjected, trying to be honest and diplomatic at once, "I'm not sure if he is."

The Landons said nothing. They looked at Casey—Janet expectantly and Steve dubiously.

"When I found Ben outside after he had stormed out of my classroom," Casey continued, "he was…" She searched for the correct word. "…distraught—out of sorts." Casey waited for

Ben's parents to voice a question, but they didn't speak. "I'm not sure if it was anger or anxiety—or a combination of both—but he wasn't controlling his emotions. I had hoped you knew." When the Landons merely glanced at each other, Janet nervously rubbing her hands together and Steve silently commanding her to be calm, Casey decided on a direct approach. "He told me about your plans to move back to Tajikistan," she explained.

"He's overreacting," Steve immediately dismissed his son's concerns, and Casey had to control the instinctive retort that came to her mind. "He should be happy about our leaving. It gets us out of his hair."

"Steve…" Janet laid a cautionary hand on her husband's leg. "Things haven't been very good between Ben and us lately," she added for Casey's benefit. "It's not easy for a boy like Ben to live with mom and dad at his age. But I think he'll come around once he realizes the positive aspects of our going back overseas."

"What are those?" Casey asked.

"Well, he'll be on his own—which is the way he likes it. He'll be able to live in a college dorm and really give soccer his full attention."

"*If* he gets a scholarship," Steve interjected.

"Of course," Janet conceded. "But he will. You know colleges have been trying to recruit him."

Steve looked at Casey. "Well, it's not going to happen if he keeps skipping school, is it."

"I don't think our greatest concern here should be Ben's scholarships," Casey said calmly. "What's going on in his mind is very serious and I think he might need help dealing with it."

Steve crossed his legs, effectively removing his wife's hand from where it rested. "We can't change our plans just because Benjamin doesn't approve of them. There's a very real need in Tajikistan that we can fill."

Janet took over where her husband left off. "Missionaries are not welcome in the country. Do you know how miraculous it is to be able to find a job and get in legally?" she asked softly.

"But with Steve's engineering, we're able to get in without any questions asked. We're so fortunate that way…"

"Ben doesn't have a problem with our leaving," Steve said, getting back to defending his plans. "He's hated living with us. This will be a relief for him."

Casey mentally referred to the journal entry she had received from Ben the day before.

*Yo, mom and dad.*

*Well done. Three kids out of your hair and two to go. At least I'll have a scholarship so I won't have to work my butt off trying to pay my bills while you're spending a year's tuition on your plane fare to Tajikistan.*

*How can you do this to the little guys? I don't care WHO is telling you to go back to that hellhole. You've got Rachel and Ian with you! It's going to kill them to go back over there. They've got friends here—and a LIFE. What? You want to see them lock themselves in their rooms for five years too? It did me a HELL of a lot of good, didn't it! And what'll you do when Rach gets old enough to be unsafe over there? She probably is already. What then? You ship her back to grandpa and grandma's and send her a card on her birthday???*

*You guys slay me. If you want to mess with your kids' minds, at least do it in a country where they belong. Don't drag them with you on another of your crappy crusades and pretend to be GOD's family serving GOD's people on GOD's mission field. Am I the only one who realizes that Rachel and Ian are god's people too? I know I'm not—but I'm pretty sure they still are…no thanks to you.*

*If I had a place to live, I'd keep the little guys here.*

*They'd be better off with this f\*\*\*\*\*-up brother than with parents who have no time for them and who couldn't care less about how GOD's will affects them.*

*You make me sick.*

*B.*

"I don't think Ben's problem is with your leaving," Casey offered his parents. "According to what he's told me, it's concern about his little brother and sister that is causing his anxiety."

"What?" Janet seemed genuinely surprised. She looked to her husband questioningly.

Casey went on. "He doesn't want them to live there. He figures they're happier here—with friends and a safe place for Rachel to grow up."

Steve was immediately defensive. "Tajikistan is a safe place. She'll just need to be careful."

"But you sent your two oldest daughters back..."

"They were careless," Janet explained. "Not at all suited to life in that culture."

Casey felt her frustration rising. "So you sent them back alone to live with relatives?"

Steve's voice was growing harder. "It was the best thing for all of us."

Casey nodded, looking from Janet's earnest face to her husband's hawkish face, wondering how two intelligent, clearly devoted people could have lost track of reality so completely.

"I don't think you're going to change Ben's mind," she finally said, bringing the topic back to the purpose of her visit. "He is devastated—angry, combative, depressed—and I really fear for his wellbeing if something isn't done to resolve this situation."

"Give him time," Steve said. "He'll get over it once he starts college and gets busy with sports."

Janet was more tactful. "It's always difficult for the children to adjust at first," she said, "but once the change happens, they really deal quite well with it."

"But Ben hasn't even dealt with the *last* change yet," Casey said, emboldened by her concern for the sensitive young man. "He might not talk about it with you, but his feelings about the years you spent in Tajikistan and the strain it imposed on the family are still raw. Your son is *hurting*. I've heard him say it and I've read it in his writing."

She paused and waited for a reaction. They looked at her as if she were speaking utter nonsense.

"I might be overstepping my bounds, here," Casey repeated, "but I sincerely think your son will self-destruct unless some kind of communication and *understanding* is restored between the three of you. I've been teaching for ten years, and I've never seen a student with so much pent-up bitterness and so completely unable to do anything with it. Can you just speak with him? Ask him how he feels about you taking your two youngest back to Tajikistan. It might not help at all, but it would at least open communication…"

"Miss Jensen," Steve said, leaning forward and bracing his elbows on his knees. "You've only been exposed to a very small part of the larger picture. Ben's feelings are not the only considerations we need to take into account. We're convinced that our presence in Tajikistan is vital. It has been so clearly divinely orchestrated that we can't deny God is in it."

"I'm not disputing that," Casey said, her voice growing a bit louder in the face of such determined denial. "I don't know enough about Tajikistan to have an opinion on whether or not your moving there again is worthwhile. All I know is Ben. And I've got to question the merits of a ministry that leaves a young man as wounded and disillusioned as he is… That boy is only about one disappointment shy of giving up on it all—God, faith, family, loyalty—and I'd hate for your departure to be the last straw. His belief in everything good is hanging by a thread, and you hold the other end of it. Let it go now, and you could lose your son." Casey realized too late that she had said more than she intended. Her compassion for Ben had pushed her to speak more honestly than a teacher should and to cross the barrier between professional and personal.

Steve sat back and quickly masked something that looked like contempt.

"We all come to faith in different ways," he said. "Ben is on a journey of his own. He'll understand eventually."

Under different circumstances, Casey might have found his statement to hold truth. But used as an excuse for deliberate neglect, it made her sick.

"I'm sorry," Casey said quietly, aware that she had probably already said too much. "That was out of line."

Ben's father stood, obviously expecting Casey to do the same. "We'll deal with Ben, Miss Jensen," he said.

Casey knew she had been dismissed. She retrieved her purse from the couch and moved to the entryway, a solicitous Janet on her heels.

"Thank you so much for coming by, Miss Jensen," Ben's well-meaning mother said. "We're grateful for your concern."

Casey opened her mouth to voice a platitude but found she had none to offer. With an uncomprehending shake of her head, she turned and left the Landon home.

## Chapter Nine

"*Bonjour!*" Casey called to the fish lady, her small victories that week lending her courage. If she could get a loaf of fresh bread out of Marthe and survive a confrontation at the restaurant, she could surely elicit an acknowledgement from the woman who used her front gate as a storefront. Casey was dressed warmly as the weather had taken a decisive step toward winter. It wasn't so much the cold as the dampness that got to her. She was grateful for a clean chimney and the warmth her fireplace provided. But the walls of her house were thick and made of solid stone. It would take many more fires to rid them of the humidity that made mold grow, paint blister, and wooden window frames buckle.

Casey was on her way to the grocery store to pick up more matches and some fire-starter cubes, but she paused for a moment by the woman standing outside her gate. She'd been taken aback by the slight change in her spirits since the evening at *Le Bigorneau*. She still struggled with the sluggishness in her mind and the weariness in her body, but there was a faint glimmer of something positive just outside her reach. She could feel it. Something about Marthe's surrender, Pierrot's friendship, Luke's encouragement and her own resilience had brought her one step closer to... But to what? Surviving? Maybe. Forgetting? No. Healing? She doubted it. Healing felt too conditional to be achieved so easily. No. This was probably just a faint brightening of the pall that had shadowed her life since Ben had...

She didn't finish the thought, forcing her mind to focus

instead on the fish lady who stood just a couple feet away, studiously ignoring her.

"Excuse me, can you tell me the name of those shellfish?" Casey asked pleasantly, pointing at the red, spider-like creatures in one of the crates.

The lady didn't answer.

"Excuse me, can you tell me the name of those shellfish?" Casey asked again, still pleasantly, still pointing.

The lady looked up and down the street in the hope a customer would appear.

"Excuse me, can you tell me the name of those shellfish?" Casey repeated again, finding warped enjoyment in trying to give a slightly different inflection to the words every time she spoke them.

The lady turned her head, glared, then faced front again. Casey felt anger combine with frustration, lending her a determination she hadn't known she possessed.

"Excuse me," she said more pointedly this time, "can you tell me the name of those shellfish?"

Still nothing from the woman wearing several layers of winter clothing over which she'd tied a bright yellow apron. Casey looked at the fish staring up at her, their mouths hanging open and their eyes glassy, and had a brief image of herself lying among them, a jubilant fish lady holding a gutting knife above her. As ridiculous as it was, the vision nearly quelled her determination, but Luke's words spurred her forward. The islanders' distaste for her was ancestral—handed down from one generation to the next—and it would fade in time. But Casey didn't know how much time she had, and she needed desperately to stop feeling like a pariah in this inhospitable place.

"Can you tell me the name of those shellfish?" she said again, hoping her persistence would take a few months off the usual time required for cross-cultural thawing. Or maybe add a few. It was a risk worth taking.

Casey's neighbor came through the hedge-trimmed gate of her property pushing a bicycle. She glanced at Casey, nodded at the fish lady, and pedaled off down the street. Casey waited until she was out of earshot before she spoke again.

"Can you tell the name of those shellfish?" She pointed as if it was the first time she had uttered the words.

"Those?" came Pierrot's voice from behind her. "Those are *araignées de mer*," he said, confirming Casey's misgivings. Sea spiders—and people actually ate them.

Unaware that he had foiled Casey's strategy, Pierrot propped himself against the fish lady's table and grinned at Casey. She had seen him a handful of times since her arrival at the Ile de Batz, and he'd been wearing this ratty navy blue sweater every time. Despite the chilly weather, he wore no jacket over it. Just his usual filthy jeans and enough dirt on his hands to make Casey want to instruct him to remove them from the fish table.

"*Va-t-en, Pierrot,*" the fish lady said, essentially telling him to get lost. She pushed him off the edge of her table and swatted him a couple times with a cloth.

"So are you buying fish?" he asked Casey, completely oblivious to the large woman still mumbling behind him.

Casey held up a finger for him to wait. She turned to the fish lady, leaned forward until she was sure she had her attention, and repeated, "Excuse me, can you tell the name of those shellfish?"

"But I already…" Casey held up her finger again, silencing Pierrot, then pointed with the same finger toward the fish lady who had become absorbed in arranging her fish for the hundredth time that day. She didn't acknowledge Casey's presence in any way.

"Hey, she's asking you a question," Pierrot said loudly, clearly impervious to the political overtones of the one-sided, repetitive conversation she was having. In his innocence, he simply assumed she hadn't heard Casey's question. When if finally dawned on him that this was a deliberate offense, he began to smile.

"*Eh, Madame Camille,*" he said playfully, "don't be mean to her! She's a friend."

The fish lady rolled her eyes.

"Seriously," Pierrot continued. "She's nice. Really."

"Tell her to go away," the fish lady said. It was the first time she had spoken since Casey had joined her at the gate. "She doesn't belong here."

"Sure she does," Pierrot corrected her.

Casey laid a hand on his arm and shook her head when he looked at her. "It's okay." He didn't need to be involved in this. Though she was grateful for his eagerness to help, she didn't want him to bear an American-loving stigma among the islanders. She regretted pulling him into it in any way.

"*Madame Camille,*" Casey said, repeating the name Pierrot had used to address her, "I know I don't belong here. And I don't understand a lot of things…" She saw no sign from the fish lady that she was listening, but plowed on anyway. "I'm sorry if my presence here bothers you, and if it will make it easier for you, I won't speak to you again."

"See? She's trying to be nice!" Pierrot interjected.

Casey tightened her hold on his arm and continued. "It's just that you sell fish right here at the bottom of my yard…"

"It's not your yard."

Casey sighed. "At the bottom of the *Kermadecs'* yard," she corrected. "And we're going to be seeing each other. If we can't be friends, can we at least not be enemies?"

Casey held the malevolent stare Madame Camille leveled at her. Everything in her commanded her to simply give up and go about her business without any thought for the belligerent fishmonger whose bright yellow apron belied a much darker personality. But she wouldn't flinch. She would hold the stare as long as it lasted, trying to infuse her own with an earnestness and willingness she didn't feel. If this was what it took to make friends in this strange place, she would play along.

It was Madame Camille who finally looked away, but Casey sensed a slight softening in her expression just before she broke eye contact.

"My name is Casey," she said. "If you ever need anything out here, just let me know." She had spoken to the side of Madame Camille's head, but she was sure the older woman had heard and understood her. With at least the beginning of a bridge built, she pulled her canvas bag higher onto her shoulder and headed to the store.

Pierrot had a different idea. He grabbed Casey's arm and pulled her in the opposite direction. "I have something to show you," he said, excitement dancing in his eyes.

"But I need to get to the store before it closes…"

"What are you buying?"

"Uhm…matches and some fire starters?" She wasn't sure where the questioning was leading.

"I've got those at the shop," he said, and Casey couldn't do anything but follow as he walked quickly down the street with her in tow.

After a couple minutes of walking, their general direction finally set off a warning bell in Casey's mind.

"Uhm… Pierrot?" she asked, out of breath from the pace of their trek.

"We're almost there," he told her.

"We're almost *where*?"

"My shop. It's right behind the restaurant. " Casey felt a moment of relief—if it was behind it, she'd be able to avoid *Le Bigorneau*. But her relief was short lived. Pierrot led her to the restaurant door and pushed it open.

"Wait a minute," she said suspiciously. "You told me it was behind the restaurant."

Pierrot assumed a longsuffering expression. "But the only way to get *behind* the restaurant," he said, "is to go *through* it."

"Oh." Casey was at a loss. Torn between seeing whatever Pierrot wanted her to see and an instinctive impulse to stay away from this place, she anchored her feet outside the door and didn't budge.

"Come on…" Pierrot pleaded.

"Pierrot," she explained miserably, "I can't go in there again. Not after what happened last time…"

His eyes widened in disbelief. "That? So you had a little thing!"

Unable to formulate an answer, Casey settled for shaking her head at her eager young friend.

"Besides," he continued, "we'll just be walking through and there's nobody here at this time of day."

"Except Marguerite," Casey mumbled.

"Nope. It's her day off."

Casey looked into his innocent face and trusted what she saw. "You're sure?"

Pierrot crossed himself. "Swear to God."

She relented. "Okay. Show me your shop."

Pierrot opened the door and trudged through ahead of her, not familiar with the niceties of a more civilized world. As soon as Casey had cleared the door, in hot pursuit of the young boy who was practically skipping through the restaurant, she saw Luke seated at the bar, exactly as he had been when she'd last been there.

She stopped dead in her tracks. "Oh."

Luke merely looked at her.

Casey felt the need to explain her presence. "Pierrot wanted to show me something in his shop," she explained in English.

Luke nodded, a slight smile lighting his brilliant blue eyes. "He showed me this morning," he said cryptically. Though his voice was typically monotone, she could tell that there was a bit of an east coast sound to his English.

"Oh."

"It's a nice one," he added, nodding his approval.

"Oh," she said again. Then added, "I'm glad you like it."

Casey was vaguely aware of Pierrot standing at the back door of the restaurant, shifting his weight from one foot to the other and fidgeting in impatience.

Luke smiled more widely. "You have no idea what I'm talking about, do you."

Casey sighed loudly. "I have no *earthly* idea!"

He jutted his chin in the direction of Pierrot's barely contained excitement. "So let him show you," he suggested wryly.

"Oh. Right." She turned and headed toward Pierrot more quickly than she needed to.

"And come back in for some coffee when you're finished." He paused. "If you'd like to."

Casey and Pierrot crossed the small courtyard behind the restaurant and entered what had once been a barn. From the moment Pierrot unlatched the large wooden door and stood aside to let Casey pass, she became enthralled with the place. When Pierrot had spoken of a shop, she had pictured a dirty, greasy auto shop with a hydraulic lift and a semi-erotic calendar on the wall. But this was a carpentry shop. It smelled of wood and was wonderfully warm thanks to the large cast-iron stove to the side of the room. There was furniture in every stage of completion on the floor and hanging from hooks on the walls—tables, chairs, dressers.

Casey had always loved the texture and vitality of wood. She loved the smell and feel of it. This place, alive with the imagining and creating of wooden pieces, was paradisiacal to Casey's mind. With a glance at Pierrot, who stood proudly at the door observing her movements and expressions, she made a slow circuit around the room, running her fingers along the beveled edge of a table, caressing the unfinished surface of a dresser with her hand. She didn't see one item that wasn't creatively conceived and flawlessly executed.

"This is your work?" she asked Pierrot, awed by the simple lines and graceful beauty of his work.

"Yeah," he said. "Mostly." His nervous twitches were getting more pronounced with every step Casey took around the shop, as if her admiration of his handiwork was a personal appraisal.

"Do you like it?" Pierrot finally asked.

"Do I *like* it? Pierrot, this is the most beautiful furniture I've ever seen! How did you learn to do this?"

"Luke taught me." He nodded toward a part of the shop where slightly different furniture was kept. "That's his over there." While Pierrot's work was immaculately finished and sometimes just a bit ornamental, the furniture on the other side of the shop looked more substantial, organic, and somehow more grounded. This was Luke's handiwork, and Casey thought she could see his bold, no-nonsense signature in the lines and shapes of his creations. She wandered closer and laid her palm flat against the surface of a solid oak table, feeling its coolness and warmth.

"He said he can't make any more until he gets a bigger restaurant," Pierrot said.

Casey put it all together.

"The furniture in the dining room?" she asked.

Pierrot nodded. "And all the rest too. The first thing he made was the bar and he just kept going after that. Now when something breaks or gets damaged or whatever, we've started putting my stuff in too."

"You're very gifted," Casey said, looking affectionately at the surprising young man. "This was definitely worth walking through the restaurant."

"But that's not really what I wanted to show you," Pierrot said, and Casey noticed for the first time that he was holding something behind his back.

"Is it something you made?" Casey asked, not sure if this was Pierrot's version of show-and-tell or if he was actually giving her something.

"I was making a chair with it," he said, excitement shining in his eyes, "but then when you said what you did the other day, I thought maybe you could use it for something else."

He brought his hand out from behind his back and Casey saw that he was holding what appeared to be the seat of a chair. She stepped a bit closer and saw the hole in the middle of the seat. Surprise, gratitude and elation sent her across the room where she embraced a suddenly awkward Pierrot and took the toilet seat he held out to her. She didn't know whether to laugh at the beautiful design or gush about it. It was solid oak and beautifully handcrafted. Pierrot had obviously modified it just a bit so it could attach to her commode, but it still looked very much like the seat of a beautiful chair.

"Pierrot..." She was out of words. "I'm going to have the happiest rear end on the island," she finally exclaimed, surprising even herself with the extent of her gratitude. "It's beautiful. Thank you."

Pierrot blushed a deep red and focused his attention on wiping sawdust off a nightstand.

Buoyed by Pierrot's gift, Casey hesitated only briefly before stepping into the restaurant again.

"What do you think?" Luke asked, looking up from his work.

"I think it's beautiful," Casey answered sincerely.

"A little unexpected?"

She laughed—and the sound brought her up short. When had she started laughing again, she wondered. A pang of irrational guilt darkened her expression.

"Can I get you a cup of coffee?" he asked.

Casey was about to refuse and excuse herself, but the thought of a hot drink made her change her mind. "I'd love one," she said, installing herself a little hesitantly on one of the tall stools at the bar.

"*Café au lait* with two sugars?"

Casey was astonished. "How did you...?"

"It's a small island," Luke answered. "And I own the place."

"The island?"

"The restaurant."

"Oh."

"That's five times you've said 'oh' since you arrived," he commented dryly, pushing away from the bar and stepping up to the coffee pot behind it.

"It's a—multi-purpose word," Casey said, a little embarrassed.

He nodded. "Is Pierrot still out there?" he asked.

"Sanding down a strange looking hollow table."

Luke smiled. "He's determined to make a foosball table."

"From scratch?"

He looked at her. "Any other suggestions?"

Casey hid her mild embarrassment behind the bowl of steaming coffee Luke handed her. She closed her eyes and inhaled the vapor, letting memories of Sunday mornings with her parents wash over her.

She heard the chimes as the front door opened but didn't look around. Luke looked over her head toward the door, nodded in greeting, then smiled as the door closed. When Casey heard no one behind her, she assumed the customer had seen her and gone.

"I'm bad for your business," she said.

Luke didn't answer. He rinsed a dishrag out in a small sink against the far wall. Casey looked above the bar to a rack of wines and liquors. She noticed colored stickers on some of the bottles' necks. There were letters written on each one of them, though they didn't seem to cover the entire alphabet.

"What are the stickers for?" Casey asked, her curiosity pushing her to be bold.

Luke followed her gaze to the bottles, then came closer to the bar and took several notebooks off the shelf beneath it. He opened one and turned it to face Casey.

"This is a cocktail recipe," she said.

He nodded. "The number of stickers beside each ingredient determines how many parts of each liquor are needed. Two stickers—two parts. One sticker—one part."

"And the letters on the stickers match the one on the bottles."

He nodded again, this time glancing toward the back door before adding, "It's a rudimentary system, but it works."

Casey followed his glance. "They're for Pierrot?" she asked.

"He tends bar when I can't be here in the evenings. We don't get a whole lot of requests for cocktails outside the tourist season, but this way he's prepared."

Casey noticed that the illustrations on each recipe matched the drawings on the cocktail menu above the bar. She assumed customers would point at what they wanted, and Pierrot would look through his recipe notebook until he found the correct drawing.

"That's ingenious," she said.

"It gives Pierrot the illusion that he can read."

"Why didn't he ever learn?"

Luke shrugged. "I don't know. He recognizes a few letters. I'm not sure his parents were very big on education."

"Do they live on the island?"

"They died a few years ago. His grandfather might as well be dead."

Casey shook her head in confusion.

"He's an alcoholic," Luke explained. "And he spends most of his time wasted and taking it out on the boy."

Casey marveled at Pierrot's enthusiasm in the face of so much sadness. "He lives with his grandfather?"

Luke sighed. "There's a cot out in the shop for when he'd prefer not to go home."

"I see," Casey said, wondering what layers of experiences lay hidden under the surface of the strangers she passed every day. "Do you think he'd be open to learning if he had the chance?" she asked with genuine interest. "I'm a teacher. Maybe I could help."

"Learning to read?"

She nodded.

"I don't know. He does alright without it," Luke replied.

Casey briefly contemplated the prospect of teaching Pierrot to read. If she could teach American teenagers how to speak French, she could surely teach a French young man to read.

At that moment, Casey realized how improbable the scene was. There she sat in a restaurant she had considered hostile until minutes before, chatting with a man she barely knew with only a twinge of self-consciousness and awkwardness. As mysterious and seemingly contradictory as Luke was, there was something about his calm confidence and straightforward gaze that quieted her usual distrust and weakened her reserve. Though the weeks preceding her arrival on the island had seen her fleeing contact with even the most well-intentioned friends and acquaintances, this man she had known only briefly was a comfortable presence, an undemanding sounding board who inspired both curiosity and trust. Her lack of fear, ironically, frightened her. She had no proof that this stranger was harmless, no assurance that he was truly what he appeared to be. Yet every instinct she possessed urged her to believe what she saw. Casey looked up and caught his unflinching gaze. She took a deep breath and returned his gaze with uncharacteristic temerity, summoning the courage to dismiss a little of his mystery.

"So I've come for coffee…"

"And a toilet seat," he interjected.

"I've come for *coffee*," she repeated, hoping he would remember the deal he had offered her as she had left several days ago.

Luke's unblinking stare considered her meaning. "And now you want to ask a few questions," he said.

Casey's resolve teetered a little. "If you're okay with it," she said.

Luke shrugged. "I'm not very good at answering questions."

"You're shy?"

"I'm stubborn."

Casey paused but wouldn't be deterred. Given the difficulty she'd had carrying on casual conversations recently, she realized she needed to take advantage of this momentary lull in her mental paralysis while it lasted.

"Where are you from?" she asked without preamble.

"Whoa there," he said, pulling up a stool opposite her at the bar and crossing his arms on its lacquered surface. He sat in silence for a moment, his eyes narrowing slightly as he looked at her. There was a glint of humor in their depths when he said, "First, I need to know how many questions you're planning on asking."

Casey raised an eyebrow. "There's a fee?"

He shook his head, smiling faintly. "I just don't talk a lot—I need to pace myself."

Casey couldn't tell if he was joking or serious, so she opted to play it safe.

"I'll have…" she made a mental inventory of her questions, "four questions."

He raised a dubious eyebrow.

"For now," Casey added.

He nodded. "Okay."

"Alright." Casey felt nervous, not so much because this man intimidated her, but because she was out of practice having normal conversations—not that there was anything normal about this interrogation. "Why do you speak English so well?"

Casey was learning to expect a nod when she asked a question. It seemed to be his way of acknowledging having heard her and buying time to formulate his answer.

The restaurant door opened again. Luke went through the same routine of nodding at his customers and smiling wryly as they left.

"My parents are American," he said as if the interruption hadn't happened.

Casey waited for more, but he volunteered no further information.

"So…did you have relatives in Brittany?" she asked, wondering how an American had ended up on the Ile de Batz.

His eyes went to the window, then back to Casey. "No."

Casey didn't know whether to find his succinct answers humorous or wasteful. "Then why did you come here?"

He paused a bit longer this time, considering her question. His eyes stared into hers, as they always seemed to do when he was thinking, and she wondered if he ever blinked.

"I was looking for something different," he finally said, then, with a smile, added, "and Mars was a bit out of the way. One more question."

There were too many mysteries still surrounding Luke for Casey to answer them all with one question.

"When did you move here?" As a final question, it was fairly lame, but it would at least set the general boundaries of his life on the island.

"Two years after my parents brought me here for a family vacation—and I've been here thirteen years since then."

Casey smiled a little shyly. "That was a long answer."

He returned her smile. "Consider it a bonus."

It was nearing dinner hour on the island, and still *Le Bigorneau* remained empty. Casey had walked by it at this hour often enough that she knew it was usually well patronized. But the tables were empty and Casey could see the elderly cook sitting on a stool at the back of the kitchen with a magazine in his hand.

Casey felt guilty for scaring away Luke's clientele and his day's income. "Is this a down night or did I scare them all away?" she asked after a moment of silence, motioning toward the empty dining room.

Luke smiled more broadly. "Oh, no. They've been around. There's been a steady stream of faces looking in through the window."

When Casey turned, she saw two heads duck out of sight. "I'm sorry," she said to Luke.

He didn't seem perturbed, but shrugged his shoulders and reached for her empty bowl.

"You realize *café au lait* is usually served for breakfast, right?"

She shook her head. "I had no idea. I had it for my first breakfast in France—after I spent the night in a hotel in Paris—and it tasted better than any of the coffee I'd had until then."

"Well, now you know," Luke said.

"Marguerite didn't seem surprised when I ordered one the first time I came here," she mused.

"Marguerite knows you're an American," he answered in his deep, monotone voice. "She wouldn't have found it strange if you'd ordered your coffee with ketchup."

Another silence lengthened as Luke took her bowl to the kitchen and came back with a rag he used to clean the counter. Casey noticed the darkness of his skin and the surprising smoothness of his hands. She expected a fisherman's skin to be calloused and rough.

Risking one more question, she said, "Do you fish much?"

Luke's hesitation to respond confirmed his previous admission that he didn't like answering questions. He took a long look at her and returned to his stool at the bar. "If I answer this one, will you let me ask a couple of my own?"

This was a dilemma. As curious as Casey was about the journey that had brought Luke to this remote island, she wasn't sure she possessed enough hindsight yet to tell him about her own. It had been a long time since Casey had answered any meaningful questions, and she feared she had lost the skills openness required. But this had been a day for taking chances. She had *almost* communicated with the fish lady and she had willingly walked back into a restaurant that had terrified her only days before. If finding out about Luke's island history required answering a couple of his questions, it was worth the effort.

She met his gaze and mentally braced herself. "Sure," she answered his question, trying to inject a confidence she didn't feel into the word.

He cocked his head to one side and looked at her from under lowered lids. "You don't sound too sure about that."

A flutter of anxiety took Casey completely by surprise. She felt inexplicably threatened. She had been doing so well with all the newness of the evening that the small reminder of her weakness unsettled her. Luke must have seen it cross her face and raised his hand to ward off her misgivings. "It's okay," he said quietly, "I know it's not easy talking about yourself. Believe me."

She felt a flush in her cheeks when she admitted quietly, almost to herself, "I can't even talk about the weather very well anymore…"

Luke propped his chin on his clasped hands, his unflinching gaze direct and honest. "How long has it been?"

Casey's instinct was to get off the bar stool and head out into the cold before the question even had time to settle into silence. She looked away from his steady gaze and willed herself not to escape. In an attempt to defer her answer, she weakly asked, "How long since what?"

His eyes were compassionate and kind. "Since whatever sent you running to this island," he said.

Casey took a deep breath. Images of her previous life flashed through her mind like the rough edit of her existence: Layle, Marilyn, Louise, Troy and the kids, Steve Landon, Janet, Ben, Ben, Ben…. Her lungs closed down over her breath and wouldn't release it. Wide eyes looked into Luke's, panic in their depths. He held her gaze and started to speak in a calm, steady voice. "I was running too when I came here," he said. "You asked if I fish. It's what I came to do," he answered her question, "but I discovered I liked carpentry better. The man who owned the restaurant hired me to build the furniture at first, then trained me to manage the business. He left the place to me when he moved into a retirement home in Morlaix. I do fish—I know you were there when I came in on the *Belle des mers* the other day—but only when one of my friends can't get out and needs me to step in for the day."

Luke's uncharacteristic monologue had given Casey time to regroup—and she knew it had been intentional—but she still couldn't muster an answer to his question. After a long silence had passed, she climbed off the tall bar stool and took a step toward the door.

"I'd get you your coat," Luke smiled, "but you never took it off."

Casey weakly answered his smile when she realized she'd been sitting there all along with her wool coat buttoned up and her canvas bag, with the toilet seat in it, on her shoulder.

"Are you alright?" he asked.

She nodded, averting her eyes. "I'm okay. Oh," she said, realizing she hadn't paid for her coffee and reaching into her bag for change.

Luke walked to the door and put his hand on the doorknob. "Never mind," he said. "This one is on the house, remember?" He pulled the door open for her and she walked out into the cold night wind.

Before he closed the door behind her, she turned to him and said in a voice barely above a whisper, "Three months."

He nodded. She knew he watched her from the doorway until she reached the bend in the road. There, she turned back and smiled as a handful of islanders came out of houses and side streets, all converging on *Le Bigorneau*.

## *Chapter Ten*

Casey was unlocking her car when Ben approached. Though the school day had been over for nearly two hours, an unexpected staff meeting had kept her long after her usual departure time. She wanted to change out of her 'teacher clothes' into something more comfortable, eat, and prop her feet up to read. Ben's appearance made her doubt that any of that was going to happen any time soon.

"Can I talk to you?" he asked, bolder in his approach than he had been before. They had spoken frequently since Casey's casual classroom comment about her faith. Ben had continued to leave samples of his writing for her to read and had even started participating more in class.

But the young man facing her in the parking lot on that day was far from pleasant. He had just come from soccer practice and his uniform was streaked with grass stains and mud. But it was his expression that caught Casey's attention. She had seen him angry, depressed, sad, hurt—but she had never seen him reproachful.

"What's going on?" she asked.

Ben seemed uncomfortable standing by her car in a busy parking lot. Casey pointed toward some steps leading up to a loading dock and Ben set off in that direction. When they were both seated, she turned to him to repeat her question.

"Ben, what's going…"

"You just *had* to talk to them," he said, anger sharpening his words.

Casey saw the tension in his jaw and the indignation in his eyes. "You mean your parents?" she asked.

"Why did you *do* that??" he asked loudly, raking his fingers through his hair as he rose and took a few steps away from Casey. He turned on her. "What did you tell them? Did you show them all the stuff I wrote in those journals??" He was frantic.

Casey stood too and took a couple steps toward him. Although his anger was virulent, she knew she had nothing to fear from him. "I didn't show them anything, Ben," she said. "I just told them that you were having trouble with their leaving."

"But I'm *not!*" he yelled. "They can go to hell and I won't mind!"

"Ben..."

"How could you tell them that?"

"What happened?"

"What happened?? I get home from soccer last night and they're waiting for me at the kitchen table—all serious and crap. And they start preaching about how god really needs them in Tajikistan and if I'm not happy about them going I'm interfering with god's will! God's *will*?" He was speaking so fast that Casey was having trouble understanding him. "Don't preach to me about god's will! What about Ian and Rachel's will, huh? What about theirs?? Nobody bothered to ask me about mine when we moved the first time because it wasn't *important!*" His words dripped with sarcasm. "What was important was their freakin' addiction to being *needed!*"

Casey drew him back to the steps, but he still didn't sit. "They really pissed me off, Miss Jensen. They really pissed me off this time."

Casey felt responsible for the family meeting that had caused such harm. "I'm sorry," she said earnestly, "I thought it would help!"

"So now I'm 'bad Ben'," he continued, "the kid who's making it harder for them to be model missionaries. Bad Ben?

Fine! I'll take it! It's a step up from being Invisible Ben!"

"When were you invisible…"

"Always!" he screamed, his eyes bright with pain and the veins in his neck standing out. "They didn't even know I existed when we were in Tajikistan. I was the kid who lived in his room and played ten-year old video games until I threw up from staring at the screen for too long. I was the boring nobody who read books and wrote and only came out to eat or to be paraded in front of their saintly missionary friends. They knew their neighbors better than they knew their own kids, and now they're telling *me* that I have a problem. *They* are my problem!!" His voice was hoarse with emotions as he frantically blinked back tears. "I hate them, Miss Jensen!" he said more brokenly than she had ever heard him. "I hate their guts."

Casey's grief was a physical pain. Ben's agony cut her deeply and filled her with overwhelming sadness. This brilliant young man with such outstanding physical and intellectual potential was being destroyed by the very ones who were supposed to be looking out for him.

"Why don't you sit down, Ben."

He sank onto the step and covered his face in shaking hands, breathing harshly and coughing as he gagged on his emotions. Unable to find words that might comfort him, Casey laid a hand on his shoulder and left it there, waiting for his breathing to quiet and his shaking to subside.

When a few minutes had passed, he wiped his face with his sleeve and looked off across the parking lot. "I'm such a loser," he said.

"You're not a loser," Casey said with all the conviction of her pain.

"Yes, I am…"

"Ben, you are an intelligent, purposeful, passionate, loyal, beautiful person and—forgive me for saying this—you don't deserve *any* of this! None of it!"

"Yes, I do," he said. His sincerity grieved and angered her.

"Why?" her voice was shrill with pent-up frustration. "Give me one valid reason why you've done anything to deserve the kind of life you've had!"

He was silent.

Casey swallowed past the lump in her throat and spoke with utter remorse. "I am so sorry, Ben. I hoped that talking to your parents might help them to see your point of view, but it backfired and you got the brunt of it. I shouldn't have gone to see them without checking with you first." She couldn't apologize sufficiently. "I am just so sorry."

He wiped his face again.

"They made it sound like I was trying to ruin their lives," he said.

"Are you?"

"No!" he answered defensively.

"Then don't worry about what they say. You know what is true about you."

She listened to Ben's harsh breathing and prayed for something restorative to say.

Ben's voice came again before she had thought of anything of value.

"How can you believe in a god who makes people hurt their own kids?" he asked.

Casey knew that every word she said next could have disastrous consequences. She thought it through carefully and decided to be bluntly truthful despite her desire to sugarcoat her response.

"To tell you the truth, Ben," she said, "the God I believe in wouldn't do that."

She gave Ben time to consider her response.

"God is a God of comfort," she continued. "He is a God who loves and protects and embraces children because they are the sum total of what humanity can be. He is a caring, attentive, and forgiving God." She paused before adding, "Don't let anyone who hurts you tell you that God told them to do it. They're lying."

"Maybe you could arrange a conference call with you, god and my parents," Ben suggested.

Casey was relieved to hear some humor returning to his voice. "Don't blame God for what Christians do to you, Ben," she implored. "We're just a bunch of idiots trying to figure things out too."

Ben nodded. "But parents shouldn't have anything to figure out. 'Take care of your kids.' Period."

Casey sighed deeply. "You're absolutely right."

"But I guess the *almighty* god should have predicted we'd screw things up when he created us to fail." He was bitterly sarcastic.

Casey felt her stomach clench with emotion. "What do you mean?" she asked, knowing full well what he was referring to.

She could sense the tension mounting in Ben again when he said, "Tell me what an intelligent god was thinking when he created a bunch of humans and said, 'Here—you get to decide if you want to be good or bad, but don't blame me if you screw up!' And then he took off into heaven and sat back while we proceeded to obliterate everything good on our planet." He looked at Casey challengingly. "Tell me how an intelligent god hatched that plan. And then tell me how he expects us not to blame him for all the crap life throws at us."

"Ben…" she began.

"Forget it," he interrupted her. "I'm not in the mood for the whole 'he didn't want us to be robots' argument. It's about as lame as the thing about our being created to praise him. Give me one good reason why I should."

Casey understood his point of view and knew there was little she could say to change it. Someone who, like Ben, had been the victim of maiming Christianity was not going to find anything worth embracing in it. "There are some things we're just not going to understand, Ben," Casey said as forcefully as she dared. "But if you focus only on those, you're missing out on what is good in faith."

Ben laughed cynically.

"Don't pay any attention to the usual debates," Casey continued, undaunted. "If scholars haven't agreed on the whole predestination and sovereignty of God issue, you're not going to figure it out either. But there is so much more to God and faith than that."

"Like what?" It was a dare for her to prove her point.

"Like the hope that pain won't win in the end. Like the security of knowing there's more to this life than our time on earth. Like the ability to make our lives and the lives of others brighter by doing exactly what the Bible tells us to do. Like the assurance that no matter how alone we are, we are never completely abandoned. Those are the promises that make it worth surviving the dark times. We know there is something *better* out there, and we know we are not alone."

"It still boils down to a lot of guess work," Ben said.

"It boils down to faith," Casey corrected him. "Choosing to believe in something we can't prove—because it improves and enriches our lives." She knew it was futile to engage him on a more theological plane. If she could just convince him that faith would improve his quality of life, the rest would come later.

But Ben wasn't willing to be convinced. "I'm not talking about this anymore," he stated.

And Casey considered the window of opportunity closed.

She offered to drive him home as they walked to her car, but he said he needed to run. She didn't question it. When they reached her car, she could tell he was struggling with something he didn't know how to say.

"What is it, Ben?" she asked.

"I'm just…" He bit his lip, choosing his words. "Why did you even stop to talk to me that day I gave you the thing about *The Little Prince*?" he asked.

Casey blinked back tears. This precious young man was

wondering why anyone would give him the time of day.

"Three reasons," she answered a bit hoarsely. "Because your mind is fascinating and honest, because my faith tells me to love and help those who need me, and because you are one of the most amazing people I've ever met. And that, my friend," she said, "is God's honest truth." She smiled. "And I'm not going anywhere."

Ben ducked his head and blushed a little. He was being sarcastic when he said, "So you listen to me because it's your duty, right?"

Casey laughed. "I'm going to assume you're intelligent enough to answer that one on your own," she said, unlocking her car and climbing inside. "I'll see you tomorrow?" she asked.

He nodded.

"I'm sorry again, Ben."

He lifted his hand in a casual wave.

Casey drove slowly from the parking lot, wondering if her interference in the Landon family had caused more harm than good. She prayed it hadn't.

∞

Casey was preparing to install her toilet seat when she heard a familiar voice outside her house. A bit surprised at her initiative—or insanity—she headed down to her gate with her toilet seat in her hand.

"Look at what Pierrot made for me," she said to Madame Camille, holding the seat at eye level so she couldn't avoid seeing it. "I'm sure he could make one for you too, if you asked him nicely enough," she added.

She could have sworn she saw a hint of mirth blending with the shock in the fish lady's eyes right before she turned and walked back up the path to her house.

An hour or so later, with her toilet seat in place and the

embers of a fire safely tucked behind her fireplace grate, Casey decided it was time to do a little exploring.

Bundled up against the cold, she walked up the hill to the semaphore, past the little store, and continued down a poorly paved road toward the east shore of the *Ile de Batz*. The houses on the Ile de Batz were mostly built in a cluster around the harbor and up the hill to the island's highest point. It didn't take long, once Casey crested that point, for the houses to become rarer and the countryside to open up into a large, flat, untamed landscape. She could see potato and artichoke fields, now resting for the winter, and in the distance, the rocky outcroppings that bordered the shore. Casey walked aimlessly, simply following the narrow road around the edge of the island. A sign pointing toward a "*Jardin Exotique*" drew her attention and took her on a short detour to the gates of a fenced-in property. Even though the gate was locked—and would presumably stay so until the tourist season began again—Casey was amazed at the lush exotic vegetation she could see through the bars. There were palm trees and cacti and other bushes and trees Casey didn't recognize. She found a small, engraved sign just to the left of the gate that described how a Parisian named Georges Delasalle had fallen in love with the island in 1897 and had made it his life's goal to cultivate an exotic oasis on the roughest part of the Ile de Batz. He had dug craters five meters deep, surrounded them with thick hedges to keep out the wind and minimize erosion, and imported the vegetation from as far away as Africa and New Zealand.

Casey made a mental note to return to the gardens when they were open for visits. She walked on along the coast, passing beaches each bearing a sign proclaiming their *Breton* names: *Porz Molloc, Porz Kavou, Porz Doun*. Some were small, secluded areas at the end of dirt paths, their dark, stony sand bearing row upon row of *goémon* seaweed brought in by the waves. Other beaches were broader, surrounded by dunes of fine white sand that sloped gracefully into the water. Casey had visions of long summer days with a book and a towel and hours to waste.

But the weather on that November day was far from clement. Dark clouds formed quickly to the north then merged into a solid front. Casey saw it moving toward the island and quickened her pace, hoping to find a road that would cut back across the fields toward home. But the faster she walked, the faster the menacing clouds seemed to advance. When the first raindrop hit her shoulder, Casey knew she was in trouble. She'd lived in the Midwest long enough to know a festering storm front when she saw it, and this one was getting ready to disgorge its poison on the island.

From the position of the church steeple off to Casey's left, she figured she'd made it about a third of the way around the Ile de Batz. The quickest route home would be across the fields. With raindrops falling more steadily and a rumble of thunder urging her on, she came to a fork in the road and turned onto a dirt path that seemed to lead in the direction of the church. The wind picked up as the storm drew nearer, and the rain, now falling heavily, became like moving sheets of water. It wasn't long before it was dripping from Casey's waterlogged hair onto her shoulders and seeping through the thick wool of her pea coat. She accelerated into a jog when she felt the first trickle travel down the skin of her back, and her breath began to come in short, sharp gasps. Her jeans, saturated with rain, clung tightly to her legs and increased the effort needed to keep up her pace.

Every time Casey squinted through the rain at the steeple, it appeared to have moved farther to her left, and when the dirt path she was on faded into a field, she realized desperate measures were in order. She scanned the horizon, looking either for a break in the storm or a shelter to hide under, but she saw neither. With a sad final look at her nearly new hiking boots, she stepped into a muddy field and set off toward the town.

She wasn't sure how long she'd been walking, but the added weight of the mud caked on her boots made it feel like she'd been out there for hours. The depth of the mud in the field made it difficult to progress quickly, but she walked at a strong, steady pace, her eyes nearly closed against the wind and rain.

The fields suddenly ended at a narrow paved road and Casey nearly cheered with relief. She set off at a trot again, quickly reaching a row of houses. She saw a wooden shelter in a paddock just off the road. It was no bigger than the fiberglass shelter in which she used to wait for her bus, but it would at least temporarily protect her from the wind and rain. Groaning from the exertion of her run, Casey climbed between the bars of the fence surrounding the paddock and stumbled under the shelter. Her breathing coming in labored gasps, she huddled against the back wall of the wooden structure and silently begged the rain to stop. When several minutes passed and the storm showed no sign of weakening, she slid down into a crouching position, wrapped her arms around her knees, and concentrated on stopping her teeth from chattering.

She was still crouching in the corner of the shelter when Luke found her. She had been weighing the pros and cons of flagging down the tractor rumbling toward the paddock on its way into town when it miraculously stopped at the gate. She recognized the worn-out sneakers as the cab door opened and the driver stepped down. Luke stood beside the ancient John Deere, oblivious to the rain, and raised his shoulders in a way that said, "Happy to see me?"

"Happy" was an understatement. Pulling her jacket off her shoulders and over her head, Casey made a dash for the paddock gate, finding it open when she reached it. Luke let her through, latching the gate behind her, then strolled to the tractor to help Casey into the cab. It was an old vehicle lacking in modern amenities, but Casey was content enough to prop herself on the slight protrusion at the back of the cab while Luke took the driver's seat and put the tractor into gear.

"Thank you so much," she said earnestly.

Luke's attention was focused on the fractions of road he could see through the windshield his wipers were barely keeping clear.

"Here," he said, aiming a vent in her direction, "this should help." Casey released a heartfelt sigh when the warm air reached her face and concentrated on trying to stop the shivers running up and down her spine.

They entered the town from the west and Luke steered the tractor toward the harbor road.

"Enjoy the walk?" he asked after a few minutes of silence.

"Right up until it turned into a swim," Casey answered. She was gratified to see Luke smile. "What brought you to the wild side of the island on a such a pleasant afternoon?" she asked, then quickly added, "Not that I'm complaining!"

Luke squinted through the windshield. "A certain guardian angel of yours."

Casey frowned. If there was a hidden meaning to his statement, she wasn't getting it.

"The kind of angel that makes toilet seats and asks every customer who comes through the restaurant if they have a blow-dryer they could loan you."

Casey was genuinely moved. "Pierrot?"

Luke nodded. "He was helping out at the semaphore when the storm hit. Thought he saw you out on the north side."

"I was a long way from the semaphore," Casey said, wondering how the boy had recognized her from such a distance.

"It's an observatory," Luke explained, and Casey realized it would be fully equipped with telescopes and other visual devices.

"Thanks for bringing out the limo," she said with a smile, her spirits inexplicably lifted by her battle against the elements and her unexpected rescue. "It's nice to ride home in style."

Luke chuckled inaudibly.

"Is this yours?" Casey asked, looking around the interior of the tractor cab.

"The neighbor's," he answered.

"But since cars aren't permitted on the island…" Casey

said, more to herself than to her chauffeur. Luke nodded confirmation. "Well, thank you, anyway," she said.

He fiddled with the vents. "Warming up?"

"It feels wonderful." As an afterthought, she added, "Now if we could just drive around for a few hours, I think I'd dry out a lot faster than sitting in front of my electric radiators."

"You don't have a fire going?"

"It's probably out by now. But I was just joking," she added, fearing he would take her up on her request and drive around the island until nightfall. "I can build one when I get home."

Luke slowed the tractor well before he got to her street and silently reversed course.

"Uhm, my house is that way," Casey said, pointing over her shoulder.

He took his eyes off the road long enough to give her an "I'm not an idiot" stare and drove on in silence. He pulled the tractor into a small barn three houses down from the restaurant and turned off the ignition. When he jumped down and held the door open, she left the warmth of the cab, shivering as the cool air immediately chilled her waterlogged clothes. Luke closed the doors of the barn behind them as they left, then led her to the restaurant.

"This way," he said when they had entered. He went to the back door, bypassing a scowling Marguerite, and held it open for Casey to go out ahead of him.

When Casey entered the shop, the first thing that registered was the comforting smell of oils, varnishes, and wood. Then she felt dry heat and headed straight for the large cast-iron stove that stood on one side of the sprawling work area. She held her hands above the hot metal and felt its warmth seeping through her skin. She stood there absorbing the heat, not realizing that Luke had left until he returned with a bundle of clothes in his hand.

He handed it to her. "Tea, coffee, or hot chocolate?" he asked.

"Oh," Casey said, taken aback.

"You're going to start that again?" He smiled.

"Start what—?" She realized what he was referring to. "Oh," she said again, then clapped her hand over her mouth. "Sorry."

"That's two."

"Hot chocolate, please," she said.

He turned and left the barn with a soft, "I'll be back in a few minutes."

Casey stepped behind a large, half-finished wardrobe and quickly changed out of her jeans, sweater, and jacket into the sweat pants and black turtleneck Luke had brought for her. She pulled his thick cotton socks over her bare feet. The clothes were comically large on her, but they were dry and wonderfully soft against her damp skin. Casey returned to the stove, pulled up a chair and straddled it, letting the fire warm her back. The heat felt absolutely divine. She crossed her arms on the back of the chair and rested her cheek against the soft wool of the turtleneck, breathing in the smell of laundry detergent and reveling in the sound and heat of the fire behind her.

Luke found her half asleep in that position when he entered with two cups of hot chocolate on a tray. He closed the shop door with his free hand, then grabbed a small end table and placed it next to Casey's chair. She stirred and opened her eyes, focusing slowly on the steaming cups in front of her.

"That smells so good," she said gratefully when her senses had returned and the smell of chocolate had swept the cobwebs from her mind. "Thank you, Luke." She reached for her cup and wrapped her hands around it, breathing in the sweet vapor.

For the first time since she'd known him, Luke looked awkward.

"You want to pull up a chair?" Casey asked.

He looked around and, locating a sturdy chair with a wrap-around backrest, carried it closer to the fire. He found a work glove and used it to open the iron doors of the stove, pushing them back until the front half of the stove was exposed. He snapped a wire grate into place in front of the flames, then installed himself in the chair.

Casey turned and faced the flames, tucking one foot under her and hugging her knee, her mug of hot chocolate close to her face. The silence stretched into minutes, but Casey felt no awkwardness. She sipped her drink and stared into the fire, feeling the tension and the chill of her adventures seeping from her.

"Do you always keep a fire going in here?" she asked after a few minutes had passed.

He shook his head. "Only when Pierrot or I are working."

"Where is he now?"

"It was me working today."

Casey stifled another 'oh' and glanced around the room. "What are you working on?" she asked.

She sensed his hesitation.

"If it's okay to ask," she hastily added, afraid that intruding on his privacy would make him even less talkative than he was.

He seemed to ponder it for a moment, then pushed out of his chair and went to the workbench on the far side of the barn. He pulled a cloth off what Casey had assumed to be a block of wood, revealing what looked like the beginning of a carving. Heedless of her sock-clad feet and the wood shards littering the floor, Casey came off her chair and approached the workbench.

She instinctively reached out a hand and traced the contours of the unfinished art, trying to piece together what she saw.

"It's not finished yet," Luke said.

"It's beautiful." She said it earnestly. Though it wasn't clear to her what the finished work would be, she was unaccountably moved by it. She looked up at Luke, surprised to see a slight flush to his cheeks. "I had no idea you were an artist."

"I'm not," he said, flicking a stray sliver of wood from the rough surface of the carving, then replacing the cloth. "I just wanted to give it a try."

"May I ask what it is?" Casey asked quietly.

He shook his head, but not in an offensive way. "I need to finish it first," he said.

Casey nodded. "Where did you learn to work with wood?" she asked, wandering back to the fire.

"Here, take this chair," Luke said. He motioned her toward his much more comfortable chair and installed himself in the one she'd been using until then. "From a man who used to live down the street from my family," he answered her question.

"Just like Pierrot is learning from you," she said.

He sipped his hot chocolate. "It gives him something to do," he said.

"He's very good. You must be a good teacher."

He shook his head at that. "He's gifted. I know several carpenters who'd hire him in a minute."

"Why don't they?"

Luke sighed. "He won't put himself out there. He figures if he can't read, he's not good enough for a real job, I guess."

Casey thought about it for a moment. "He's an intelligent kid," she said. "If he would just give it a chance, I think I could probably teach him the basics."

Luke smiled and looked at her. "If anyone can convince him, I think it's probably you."

She felt herself blushing and took another sip of her drink to hide her face. "He's a sweet boy," she said, tucking her foot under her again.

"The Ile de Batz mascot," he said.

Casey smiled at that. "What does he do when he isn't helping you?"

"He helps Roland with the ferries when they dock. Helps out at the semaphore, mostly cleaning the windows and keeping an eye out for lost foreigners…"

"Hey," Casey said mock-defensively, "don't you turn on me too!"

He chuckled. "Made enough enemies already, huh?"

She sighed. "You know, I appreciated your optimism the other night, but I'm not foreseeing any immediate thaw. I even showed Madame Camille my toilet seat and she didn't crack a smile."

"No, but she did come in here and tell Pierrot he did a good job."

"Are you serious?"

He nodded. Casey was mildly surprised. "That was almost kind of her," she said.

"Everybody loves him around here," Luke answered. "Especially the ones who know his grandfather."

"What's he like?"

"He's an ornery old coot. Spends his time shooting seagulls from the windows in his attic. The only reason there hasn't been an accident is that he's usually too drunk to be conscious for long."

"Isn't it illegal to shoot a rifle in the middle of town?"

Luke nodded. "And to shoot seagulls. But he's an islander. He's an obnoxious old drunkard, but they would never turn him in. He's one of them."

Casey asked the question that had been on her tongue for several days. "So how did they react to you when you first came?"

He raised an eyebrow.

"You were an American. An *invader*. Did they try to run you out of town too?"

He shook his head, taking a sip of his drink and waiting a few moments before answering. "They didn't know I was American until I'd been here for a few years," he said. "My accent is good enough that it didn't give it away. They assumed I was a *Parisien* moving to the island on a whim. They usually don't last long here. So the islanders just sat back and waited for me to get sick of the weather and sick of them."

"But you didn't."

He allowed another silence to lengthen. Casey didn't push him, knowing the answer would come when he was ready.

"By the time I moved to the Ile de Batz, I was pretty sure I didn't deserve to be treated any better than I was."

Casey's mind buzzed with follow-up questions she didn't dare to voice. She hoped he would say more if she just waited long enough.

"And then I met Lucien," he said after a long pause Casey had assumed to be final. He looked at her, "The owner of this place." Casey nodded her understanding. "And I guess he decided he needed an heir and I was it."

She smiled at the serendipity. "I love it when things just come together," she said.

"Well, they didn't just slide into place either. There were some unhappy people around here who thought the restaurant should go to someone who was from the island. His family put up a bit of a legal fight too, but he hadn't seen any of them in years and the court dismissed their case pretty rapidly."

"How long ago was that?"

"Twelve years."

Casey had to ask. "Are you happy here?"

His gaze left the fire and met hers. He nodded. "I am."

"You seem content," she said—and surprised herself by articulating the thought. She realized she felt a tiny pang of jealousy at his serenity.

His eyes were still on hers as he considered her statement, then nodded. Looking back to the fire, he said, "It took me a while to get there."

"And a bit of good luck," she said, referring to his family's discovery of the island and his inheritance from Lucien.

He shook his head. "Divine intervention," he said, refuting the concept of luck.

Casey was so taken aback that she wondered if she'd heard him correctly. To confirm it, she repeated, "Divine intervention?"

He nodded and met her gaze. "There isn't a whole lot in this life that's left to chance," he said. "It's mostly choice and consequences."

Something in her subconscious darkened her expression. He saw the change.

"Something I said?" he asked.

She shook her head. "I was just thinking that some choices only have secondary consequences."

"Meaning…"

"They seem to affect everyone *but* the person who made the decision." She shook her head again. "It's not important."

He turned in his chair and faced her, resting his elbows on his knees, his mug still in his hands. "What are you running from?" he asked. His voice was soft, compassionate.

Casey tried to feign ignorance, but alarm clouded her gaze. "I don't know what you mean," she said, looking down.

The silence deepened. Luke turned his head toward the fire but said nothing. Casey stared at her empty mug and willed herself not to contemplate the circumstances that had brought her here. When she could stand the silence no longer and in a desperate attempt to shift the conversation toward safer subjects, she said, "You never told me why your French is so perfect. Even after several years, an American shouldn't speak as well as you do."

She could tell from Luke's silence that he was contemplating whether to press her further or allow the change of topic.

"I grew up in France," he finally said.

Casey sighed quietly, relieved that the moment was over.

"My parents moved here right before I was born," he added, letting Casey know that the conversation was safe again.

She nodded, as much at his statement as in acknowledgement of his kindness. "So you attended French schools?" she asked.

"Then boarding schools. From the age of twelve."

Casey frowned. "Twelve." She pictured Luke as a sixth grade student and couldn't imagine him being left to fend for himself in a boarding institution. "Why did your parents send you away?"

He smiled and didn't answer. Casey got the message: this was a conversation best left for another time.

"Was it hard? It *had* to be…" She couldn't help herself. Her mind was still on the little boy with the big, scared blue eyes.

Luke sighed heavily and turned back to the fire. "Actions and consequences," he said softly.

Casey observed him quietly, looking for a trace of anger or bitterness in his expression and finding none. She quelled an impulse to condemn his parents and settled instead for a less personal tack.

"What did your parents do in Paris?" she asked.

He finished his hot chocolate and leaned back in his chair.

"They were missionaries," he said.

## *Chapter Eleven*

*Hey, god.*

*If you're there, knock twice. Just joking.*

*I had an interesting conversation with my parents today. They figured since our last one didn't go that well, they would try a different approach. So instead of convincing me of the "eternal value" of their years in Tajikistan, they decided to convince me that I was going to hell. They were pretty subtle about it, but I've heard the general concept often enough that they didn't have to hit me over the head with it.*

*This is my theory: They think that if I could just "accept Jesus into my heart", I would suddenly understand why it's a good thing to sacrifice children on the altar of missions. (No offense.)*

*They still think my problem is that I'm worried about not having them around next year. I don't care how many times I try to tell them that it's Ian and Rachel I'm worried about…they want it to be about me. Ben's the guy with the problems. Ben's the guy who needs extra prayer. Ben's the black sheep who didn't quite turn out the way he was supposed to. Wrong—I'm just the one who doesn't care if they know how messed up I am. Angela is scared of her own shadow (you can thank our Muslim friends for that) and Susan thinks she needs to rule the world if she's going to survive it, but nooooo...they're not messed up. As long as they say their prayers, right?*

*So this is the deal, god. You know all those times I raised my hand when everybody's heads were bowed and the church sang "Just as I Am"? And the times I went up to the front of the church with all the other sinners and prayed with some dude who had onion breath? Those times didn't work. Well—I'm assuming they didn't work since I wasn't one of the few who heard "The Call" to Tajikistan. My parents don't think so either, because they asked me today to "surrender my will" (huh?) and then it would all make sense. So I guess that's what I'm doing. I'm surrendering my will. Like I've ever had one. They're the "grown-ups" and I'm the insignificant problem child. But if there's even a micro-whatever of will in there, it's yours—on a proverbial platter. Go ahead. Send them back to Tajikistan and let them save the sinners. I'm not going to put up a fight.*

*Can I ask you one thing, though?*

*Keep an eye on Rachel and Ian. Those Christians, you know. They'll mess a kid up.*

*Over and out. Radio-silence begins now.*

*B.*

"You're coming with me," Marilyn said.
She grabbed Casey by the arm and pulled her across the

front office and through the door into the principal's office. He was long gone as the school day had ended quite a while ago.

"Wow," Casey said, "it's been a while since I was dragged into the principal's office. Do I have to turn in my friends who smoke in the bathroom?"

Marilyn smiled, but her eyes were serious. Casey was instantly concerned.

"What's going on?" she asked.

"Honey, I hate to be the one to break this to you, but somebody's got to."

Casey wondered if she should sit before the punch line. Though Marilyn looked somber, she didn't have the expression of a person bringing tragic news, so Casey hoped she would be fine standing.

"You know how the rumor mill works around here, right?"

Casey nodded. If this was about the rumor mill, she could deal with it.

"Well, you've been a regular topic lately."

Casey laughed. "Marilyn, the kids have made up stories about me ever since the first day I set foot in the school. I've been married about a dozen times and I think there was something about having had a sex change operation that surfaced about this time last year. Let them talk!"

"Except that it involves a student this time."

Marilyn's statement put an abrupt end to Casey's good spirits. Her eyes narrowed and her blood ran cold. "Ben?"

Marilyn nodded. "I'm not sure if it started with the kids or with the staff, but it's made the rounds."

"How bad?"

"Oh, everything from giving him his tests in advance to having an illicit romance…"

"What?!"

"A secret romance…"

"I know what 'illicit' means, Marilyn. I just can't believe

they'd stoop that low!"

Casey dropped into one of the chairs facing the principal's desk and Marilyn slid into the other.

"I'm really sorry," Marilyn said.

Casey looked into her friend's eyes and was horrified to see a question there. "Marilyn!" she said, dismay in her voice, "you don't believe them, do you?"

Marilyn looked instantly contrite. "Honey, it's just that there are elements of truth."

Casey rested her elbow on the arm of the chair and rubbed her forehead in frustration. "I can't believe this."

"I've delivered quite a few papers to you over the past few weeks, and I'm pretty sure they weren't all homework."

"He's a *student*, Marilyn!"

"And you're a young, attractive woman…"

"I am *not* a pedophile!!"

Casey's last word seemed to hang in the silence that filled the office. Marilyn looked down at her hands and Casey continued to stare at her in disbelief.

"If there was even a shred of truth to the rumors," Casey said, "I would have *myself* arrested."

"You do spend a lot of time talking with him…"

"Correction," Casey interrupted angrily. "*He* talks to *me*. And we don't sit around and compare life stories. These are conversations that need to happen."

"About school stuff?"

"No, Marilyn," Casey said with tenuous patience. "About him. He's been through a heck of a lot more than you or I have, and he needs to be able to express it to someone."

"But why to you? With all the male teachers in this school, why do you think he chose the pretty French teacher?"

Casey was astounded. "Because he knew I'd listen?" she suggested. "Because I like his writing? Because he figured I'd understand?" She sighed. "I don't know why he chose me, Marilyn, I just know that he did! What am I supposed to do now—

pass him off to someone else?"

Marilyn shook her head and smiled sadly. "I don't know what to tell you," she said. "Maybe you could ask a male teacher to take over…"

"And then what? Go to Ben and say, 'Hey, thanks for trusting me, but we can't talk anymore because people might think I'm molesting you'?" She waited for a response that didn't come. "I suggested that he talk to the school counselor last week and he refused. I can't impose it on him—not yet." She took a calming breath. "This is a kid who was a flatline until two months ago. And then one day, because of a comment I made in class, he decided to vent a little. And when he saw that I was listening, he vented a little more. And when I didn't tell him to take a flying leap, he got down to the real stuff—the life and death stuff—and he saw that I didn't go running in the opposite direction. And now this kid who has trusted *no one* since as far back as he can remember is spilling his guts and asking his questions of me. That's not something you *pass off* to someone else. That's something you *thank God* for!"

"I just think…"

"The moment he's open to talking to someone else, I'll gladly set it up. Believe me, I don't *want* to be the only person he talks to, but there's nothing I can do until he's ready."

"And what about the fallout?"

Casey felt a rush of defiance. "I'll deal with it," she said, then sharply asked, "Who is saying these things?"

Marilyn thought for a moment, unsettled by her friend's anger. "Some of the soccer guys—their coach told me about it. And I've heard a couple snide comments in the staff room…"

The rumors were nauseating. Casey shook her head in utter revulsion and went to the window that overlooked the parking lot.

"What am I supposed to do?" she asked, turning to her friend. "They're questioning my integrity. I could get fired for this kind of rumors!"

"Could you just scale it back a little?" Marilyn asked quietly.

"Scale it back." Casey laughed bitterly. "If it *was* an illicit romance," Casey said angrily, "I could scale it back. This boy needs someone desperately, Marilyn."

"Does it have to be you?"

"Ask him! This was not my choice! But now that he's started to talk, it's my *responsibility* to be there. I am *not* going to break my promises to him."

Marilyn wasn't able to mask her qualms.

"What?" Casey demanded.

"What kinds of promises have you made?" Marilyn asked, clearly dreading her friend's answer.

Casey shook her head and released a defeated breath. If even Marilyn doubted her motives, there would be no winning back the trust of other staff members and students.

"I told him I wasn't going anywhere," she said, walking to the door. Then, with her back to Marilyn, she added, "Every adult in his life has betrayed him—I'm not going to be the next one."

She walked out.

There were two more words carved into the cover of the black notebook than there had been the first time Ben showed it to her. Casey carried it to the big leather chair in the living room and, sitting, placed it on her lap. It now read, "Book of F*****-Up Confusion", the two extra words added above the previous title. She had held the notebook in this manner on frequent occasions, tracing the indentations of the title with her fingers and imagining a human warmth emanating from its surface. On courageous days, she had gone as far as to slip a hand between the pages, feeling the shallow ridges created by Ben's heavy penmanship. But she hadn't yet allowed herself to read from the notebook. It would have sealed a reality she wasn't ready to accept.

But with thousands of miles separating Casey from the suburban fishbowl of Glen Ellyn, she chanced to open the notebook for the first time. Just weeks before, such an act would have sent her reeling for hours, prey to the torture of second-guessing that had tormented her night and day for months. Though she didn't look at the pages she turned—she couldn't read them yet—she leafed through the book, concentrating on the static in her mind. Would it rear up and incapacitate her again? Would she be precipitated back into shrieking condemnation and succumb once more to the chaotic darkness?

Casey allowed herself a wistful smile when she reached the middle of the notebook and perceived no immediate threat to her emotional stability. Though sadness overwhelmed her, panic did not. She hadn't dared to hope for a reprieve from her relentless guilt and grief, yet it seemed an infinitesimal stirring of healing had begun in spite of her self-flagellation and remorse. She contemplated the influences that had brought her to this slightly lighter place.

The doorbell rang, startling Casey out of her reverie. She quickly slipped the notebook into a drawer in the buffet and headed for the front hallway. Pierrot stood on the stoop and Casey wondered, given his pleased-as-can-be expression, if he had made her another toilet seat.

She looked at him with suspicion. "You're hiding something behind your back, aren't you."

He nodded vigorously.

"And I already have a beautiful hand-made toilet seat, so this must be…" She raised her eyebrows expectantly and waited for Pierrot to fill in the blank.

He hopped a little on the balls of his feet, then triumphantly extended a blow-dryer to her.

"Where did you find it?" she exclaimed, taking the blow-dryer into her hands as though it were made of gold.

"Marguerite," he said.

"Marguerite??"

"She said if I tell you she'll kill me," he added conspiratorially. "She just gave it to me so I'd stop asking her about it."

Casey smiled broadly. "It'll be our secret."

"Cool."

Moved by the young man's repeated kindness, Casey asked earnestly, "Pierrot, what can I possibly do to repay you?"

He blushed furiously and Casey's suspicions were aroused. Her years of teaching had taught her that this was the look of someone who didn't know how to ask for a favor.

"Or do you already know how you'd like me to repay you?" she added.

The boy blushed a shade darker and didn't make eye contact. After an interminable silence, he finally mumbled, "Luke said you're a teacher."

Elation surged through Casey's mind, but she kept it strictly under control, unwilling to let it dismantle Pierrot's boldness.

"I am," she said as casually as she could, trying to sound at once confident and unintimidating. When Pierrot merely shuffled his feet and stared at her doorstep, she added, "Is there something you would like to learn?"

He shrugged. "Maybe if you could, uhm, you know…"

"Teach you to read?" Casey finished softly.

He nodded vigorously.

Casey reached out and touched Pierrot's chin, lifting it until his eyes met hers. "Pierrot, there is nothing I would love more than to teach you how to read," she said earnestly.

"Really?" He seemed amazed by her easy agreement.

"How about starting this afternoon?" she asked, a lesson plan already forming in her mind.

Fear and excitement dueled in the young man's gaze. "I meet the ferry at five."

"Then we'll work until four thirty," she said, knowing an hour or so of learning would be more than enough for his first day. "And if you like it, we can meet every afternoon for an hour or so. How does that sound?"

"Really?" he asked again, pure, undiluted joy lighting his face.

Casey nodded and felt something come alive in her. Though teaching had held its share of challenges and frustrations, it had always been her passion. The prospect of being able to teach this gifted young man the rudiments of reading was a jolt of energy to her brain.

"Give me a few minutes to get ready, and we'll start right away."

"Here?" Pierrot asked, looking a little awkward about entering her home.

Casey understood his reservation. If fear of humiliation had kept him from learning for so long, she needed to teach him in a place that felt comfortable and safe.

"Do you think we could use the shop?" she asked.

His shoulders relaxed visibly as she made the suggestion. He nodded vigorously again and tried to mask an ecstatic grin.

Casey didn't bother to hide hers. With a glance at her watch and an eagerness that matched Pierrot's, she said, "I'll see you there in a half hour."

"Cool," he said. He seemed glued to the spot.

"Cool," Casey repeated with a laugh.

He stood there and stared excitedly at his new teacher for a moment longer, then swiveled on his heels and bounced down the steps and all the way to the gate. He punched the air with an exuberant fist and said another loud "Cool!" as he ran down the street toward *Le Bigorneau*.

∝

Life settled into a routine for Casey. She spent time every morning preparing her lessons—which required some advance planning since there were no textbooks or curriculum—and every afternoon found her in the shop with Pierrot. The boy learned fast and rose to every challenge with enthusiasm. He had a rudimentary knowledge of some of the alphabet, and his keen mind quickly assimilated the combinations of vowels and consonants. With reading coming along so easily, they decided to extend the lessons to writing as well.

Three weeks after they had started the lessons, Pierrot turned up with an armload of books he had borrowed from islanders and declared that he wanted to read them all. Casey laughed and encouraged him to be patient. She selected short passages from the books and carefully guided her enthusiastic young student through them, finding her own teaching skills challenged by his eagerness to learn.

At four thirty every weekday, he would thank her for the lesson and take off at a jog toward the harbor to help with the incoming ferry. Casey would tidy up the "teaching area" they had created in a corner of the workshop and brace herself to cross Marguerite's path as she passed through the restaurant on her way home. On the days when Luke was there, he would offer her a cup of coffee or hot chocolate, and they would sit at the bar discussing Pierrot's progress and island events—the wind damage caused by storms, the passing of a patriarch, economic concerns, and facts about the quirky islanders' lives.

It was from Luke that she learned about the island's superstitions and its inhabitants' fervent belief in bad omens, ghosts, and mediums. He told her that a sailor's greatest fear was finding anything to do with rabbits aboard his ship. Centuries before, ships that had set sail with stowaway rabbits onboard had quickly became overrun with the rodents. When they found that they were trapped, the rabbits resorted to gnawing through the wooden structures of the ship to escape, eventually making holes in the hull and causing the vessel to sink. To this day, a toy rabbit or any form of rabbit meat found on a ship spelled bad luck and could cause a captain to reverse course.

Although their general behavior toward Casey didn't change, she felt a subtle alteration in the islanders' coldness. Perhaps it was caused by Pierrot's enthusiastic reports about the progress he was making with his teacher, or maybe it was her resiliency in the face of their nastiness. Whatever it was, Casey found herself not taking their gruffness so personally and rejoicing in the smallest signs of a thaw: conversations that didn't completely come to a standstill when she entered the island store, eye contact with Marthe when she stopped in at the *boulangerie* for her customary loaf of bread, and elderly gentlemen who didn't change sidewalks when they crossed her on the street. Relations with the island's natives were still far from friendly, but their inhospitality and muteness had become somehow more bearable.

Casey always left the restaurant before the evening patrons appeared, unwilling to be responsible for depriving Luke of business. She found herself looking forward to the conversations she had with him when Pierrot had gone off to the harbor—and deeply disappointed when they didn't happen. Every hour spent sitting across the bar from him increased her comfort level in his presence and allowed for a deeper conviction of his sincere kindness and her ability to trust him.

On one particularly blustery Friday afternoon when Luke had gone to Roscoff to pick up supplies, Casey bought another phone card and installed herself at a pay phone in the post office lobby.

"Hello?"

It had been weeks since Casey had heard Layle's voice, and the familiar sound brought a lump to her throat.

"Hey," she said, willing her voice to be steady so as not to alarm her protective sister.

"Casey!" came Layle's immediate exclamation.

"It's so good to hear your voice," Casey said with genuine feeling.

"Yours too," came Layle's voice, just as rough with emotion as Casey's was. "I've been worried."

"I know," Casey said, realizing she had been so self-absorbed that she hadn't thought of the effect her silence would have on her sister. "I'm really sorry. I should have called sooner."

"You sound…" There was silence on the other end of the line while Layle looked for the right words, "You sound *okay*," she finally said.

Casey contemplated her sister's assessment. Was it possible that her time on the island had changed her enough that her sister could hear it? The possibility raised her hopes but also filled her with guilt. It felt too soon for her to be healing. There was too much still dreadfully wrong with her world.

"Well, I'm probably a bit more 'okay' than the last time we spoke," she conceded, uncomfortable with the admission for reasons she didn't want to ponder. "How are the kids and Troy?" she asked.

If Layle sensed her evasive technique, she didn't comment on it. "They're doing great," she said. "Toby's in the den watching Nemo for the hundredth time and Melissa's at school."

Casey could picture Toby curled up in the armchair, staring at the screen with wide, innocent eyes. She missed his simpleness.

"How are *you* doing?" Layle asked. "You've been there forever."

Casey sighed. "It sure feels like it."

"Is it beautiful? Are the people nice? Are you keeping yourself busy?"

Casey laughed. "Well, if you like wind and rain, it's beautiful. If you like obnoxious people, I guess you could say they're nice. And if building fires, taking long walks, and teaching a seventeen year old boy how to read and write counts as being busy, then yes—I am."

"It's good to hear you laugh," Layle said quietly. Then, more loudly, "Wait—what's this about building fires?"

Casey explained about the small radiators and their inability to heat her house, then went on to elaborate about her general living conditions. "I'm not complaining," she concluded, "but I'm starting to understand why Louise's family uses it as a *summer* home. There are days when I'd give anything for my furniture, my bathroom, and my central heating."

She guessed Layle's next question before she posed it. "Are you going to stay there much longer?" her sister asked.

It was the first time Casey had considered the length of her stay. When she had left the States, her end goal had been getting away. Since her arrival on the island, her goal had been everyday survival. Now, her life revolved around teaching Pierrot, cohabitating with the islanders, and talking with Luke. *Talking with Luke*, she mused. When had that become a priority.

"I'm not sure," she told her sister, for lack of a more precise answer. "I'm playing it by ear."

"Oh," Layle said, and Casey smiled. *That's one*, she could hear Luke say.

"Please don't worry about me, Layle."

There was a pause. "Okay," her sister conceded. "Just let me know if you need anything."

They talked for a few more minutes, Layle catching Casey up on the news from Glen Ellyn and Casey describing a little more about life on the island. When they hung up, Casey sat by the phone, deep in thought, until the postmaster informed her he was locking the doors.

Casey was in the staff lounge when Marilyn came in with her daily delivery of papers and mail. The two women hadn't resolved their differences since their discussion in the principal's office, and there was a conspicuous tension between them as

Marilyn stuffed the teachers' mailboxes. She handed Casey a piece of paper that had obviously been torn from a bound notebook and moved to sit in the chair across from her.

"I shouldn't have doubted you," she said.

Casey looked up from her reading and met her friend's gaze.

"And you're right," Marilyn continued, "It *is* your integrity they're questioning. But I've known you too long to distrust you on something like this." She paused. "I'm sorry for being suspicious."

Casey sighed deeply. "I'm not doing anything wrong, Marilyn," she said, her eyes showing the pain of the accusations against her.

Marilyn nodded. "I know that—and you know that," she said. "Are you willing to let others think differently?"

Casey hesitated only briefly. "I'd have to break Ben's confidence to set them straight," she said with determination. "So yes. I'm happy to let them have their sick theories. If any of them care to ask, the truth is on my side."

Marilyn patted her friend's knee and stood. "I'll have your back," she said.

Casey laughed at that. "What—are we trapped in a bad cop show or something?"

Marilyn laughed too. "You know what I mean."

"I know what you mean."

"See you at the game?"

Casey had forgotten about it. "I'll be there."

"Good. I'll be the fatso on top of the cheerleaders' pyramid." Marilyn wiggled her fingers at Casey and left the staff lounge.

As soon as the door closed behind her friend, Casey opened the paper she had been holding. It was written in Ben's sharp handwriting and dated that same day.

*Ode to Oblivion*

*I tried to run and found my flight impeded*
*I tried to learn but couldn't comprehend*
*I tried to scream and found my cry unheeded*
*I tried to die but survived in the end*

*I tried to love but found more peace in hatred*
*I tried to hope but found no comfort there*
*I tried to trust but found it left me naked*
*I tried belief but found only despair*

*So I dismiss the insult of salvation*
*And I regret the time I lost for god*
*I join the brokenness of his creation*
*And long to find my rest beneath the sod*

Casey read the poem three times. She walked to the window and read it again. Unwilling to act in panic, she considered the message of Ben's poem and the lines of action she should take. Professional ethics demanded that she report her fear that Ben might harm himself.

She walked to Marilyn's office on leaden legs and asked to see Ben's schedule. Marilyn saw her expression and didn't question her request. When Casey reached the physics lab, she saw no sign of Ben. A quick conversation with the teacher confirmed that he was supposed to be there but hadn't shown up.

She returned to Marilyn's office and her friend didn't hesitate when Casey asked to see the principal. Marilyn knocked on his office door and opened it. "Mr. Evans," she said calmly, interrupting the meeting he was having with a prospective student and her family, "Miss Jensen needs to see you immediately."

Principal Evans asked the family if they would wait for him outside and apologized for the interruption. As soon as the door had closed behind them, Casey handed him the paper bearing Ben's morbid poetry. He sat at his desk, donned his bifocals, read the poem once, and then more carefully a second time.

"Give me some background," he said, looking up at Casey.

"Ben has been sharing quite a bit of his writing with me lately," Casey began, her voice a bit unsteady. "It's been angry and unhappy, but never this overtly suicidal. I received this one just a few minutes ago."

The principal removed his glasses and released a deep breath. "What's your assessment?" he asked.

Casey hesitated. "He's a sensitive kid," she said. "If this is nothing, whatever we do will only compound his problems with authority figures." She chose her words carefully. "But I just checked with his physics teacher and he didn't turn up for class. I don't think we should ignore this." She looked directly at the principal. "I'm afraid he's capable of harming himself."

The principal punched the intercom button and asked Anna for the Landon's home phone number and the school's attendance record for that day. As soon as she gave them to him, he dialed and turned on the speakerphone.

"Mrs. Landon?" he asked when she picked up.

"Yes."

"This is Principal Evans at Glen Ellyn High. I'm calling about Ben."

"Yes, Mr. Evans. Is there a problem?"

"Mrs. Landon, your son is missing from his class."

An exasperated sigh came from Janet Landon's end of the line.

Principal Evans continued. "I have a sample of some of

your son's poetry in front of me, and one of his teachers and I are concerned that he might be considering harming himself."

"Oh dear," Janet said mildly. "Ben has always been a bit dramatic, Mr. Evans. He might be skipping out on his class, but I don't think he would do anything to harm himself."

The principal looked closely at the attendance record. "Our records show that Ben never made it to his first class this morning—or any after that."

"Really?" She sounded more annoyed that worried. "We'll have a talk with him about that, Mr. Evans. I promise you it won't happen again."

The principal looked at Casey incredulously. "Mrs. Landon," he said more firmly, "do you have any idea where your son might be right now?"

There was a brief silence. "Let me ask my husband," she said quickly.

Casey heard the sound of the receiver being put down. A few moments later, Steve Landon's voice came across the phone line.

"Mr. Evans?"

"Yes, Mr. Landon. Has your wife filled you in?"

"She has," he said curtly. "I'd appreciate it if you could have a look around the school grounds, and I'll do some calling from this end."

"Would you like us to contact the police?" the principal asked, looking at Casey as he addressed the question to Steve Landon.

After a brief hesitation, Ben's father answered, "Not yet." He tersely added, "I'll call you back in a few minutes."

"Incredible," the principal said after he had hung up the phone, his frustration obvious. He looked up at Casey. "What do you think?"

She felt a shiver of fear. "What's the usual procedure?" she asked.

"Follow the parents' lead until we have good reason to do otherwise."

Casey nodded. "Then we should search the school," she said.

In a matter of minutes, members of the staff and faculty had been mobilized and assigned areas of the school grounds. Only Ben's closest teammates were pulled from their classes and questioned by Casey and Principal Evans. None of them knew where he was. Teachers and staff members began to return from their searches without having found Ben.

On an impulse, Casey asked the principal if anyone had been asked to search the soccer field. No one had. They took off at a fast pace toward the field on the East side of the school. There was no one on the field and no one in the stands. They were about to head back to the office and call Ben's parents again when he came strolling out of the woods on the far side of the field.

Principal Evans saw him first. Casey followed his gaze and nearly wept with relief. A thousand thoughts went through her mind—all concluding that he was alive and that that was all that mattered. They met in the middle of the field.

"You've caused quite a stir around here," Mr. Evans said to the student who stood defiantly in front of him, looking him square in the eyes.

Ben shrugged. Anger flashed in the principal's eyes. He turned to Casey. "I need to get back and call his parents," he said, silently passing the baton to her. She nodded. Looking at Ben again, he said, "You need to come to my office as soon as you're finished here. Your parents and I will want to talk with you." He turned and walked toward the school.

Casey stood mutely with her student while her heart rate slowed and her fear subsided. It was replaced with an overwhelming relief that converted into rage.

"What were you thinking?!" she demanded when she trusted her voice enough to speak.

Ben shrugged.

"No," she said forcefully, shaking her head in frustration,

"you don't *get* to shrug, Ben. Not after what you've pulled this morning."

"What?" he asked caustically. "I just went out to the woods for a smoke. There's no crime in that."

Casey took a calming breath and struggled to control her anger. She hadn't seen him this defiant before and suspected that he had caused the uproar deliberately.

"Why did you do it?" she asked.

"I felt like smoking," he answered, intentionally misunderstanding her question.

"You knew that your poem and your absence would send up enough red flags to set the school and your parents scrambling," she accused.

He stared her down in silence for a moment then turned his gaze pointedly to the empty soccer field. "Parents?" he asked, a bitter smirk curving his lips.

"Why?" she pleaded, her anger finally ceding to weak disbelief. Her fear for his welfare had drained every ounce of strength from her body and all she wanted now was an explanation.

She didn't get one. Ben stood there silently. Casey was vaguely aware that he didn't smell of cigarette smoke.

"When did you write the poem?" she finally asked, desperate to establish some form of real communication with the boy.

"Last night," he said. "This morning," he amended.

"Which is it?"

He looked at her. "Around four a.m."

She nodded. "What were you doing awake at four a.m.?" She tried to sound calm enough that he wouldn't react to the emotion overwhelming her.

He shrugged again, and Casey felt the urge to grab his shoulders and shake some sense into him—or embrace him. Tears of fear, relief, and affection welled in her eyes. Ben saw them and looked away, a muscle working in his jaw.

"Well, if you wanted to get your parents' attention," she said after a minute had passed, "you succeeded." She wondered if her statement was truthful. They had shown no sign of significant worry.

He said nothing.

"And you scared *me* to death," she added, emotion tightening her voice.

"I didn't mean to," he said, and she believed the authenticity of that statement.

While he was being truthful, she decided to push her luck. "How serious was that poem, Ben?" she asked.

He looked out over the soccer field and she wondered how peculiar they must look, the teacher and the student standing still in the middle of a deserted field, making eye contact only occasionally.

He stuffed his hands into his pockets. "It was serious at four a.m. this morning," he said.

"And now?"

He shrugged.

"I need you to make me a promise, Ben." She took a step that placed her in her student's line of vision. "If you start to feel that way again, call someone. Immediately. And if you choose to show me more poetry like what I read this morning, give it to me in person."

He held her gaze.

"And don't you *dare* kill yourself." She hadn't intended to say the words, but they held all the anguish and love this broken young man evoked in her. She wasn't aware of the tears pooling in her eyes or the tremor in her voice when she added, emphasizing each word, "Life—will—get—better. I can't prove it to you now, but you have to take my word for it."

His defiance weakened. Discomfort at her tears—and a hint of remorse—replaced his belligerence.

Casey laid a hand on his arm. "And about the poem?"

He nodded.

"Stop trying to prove God. And stop trying to disprove Him. And stop judging Him by how your parents and others have treated you." She looked directly into his eyes with all the conviction her shredded emotions could muster. "Embrace what you can know of Him, and let the rest go. Let *people* be responsible for their mistakes. Not God. He didn't do any of this to you." Ben looked away, before she added, "It seems to me He's all you've got left."

Ben turned away from Casey and took a few steps toward the school. She could see teachers gathered on the front porch and knew the time she was spending with Ben would fuel more rumors. When Ben was a few feet in front of her, without turning back, he stopped and said, "If anyone hurt me, it's because god gave them the capacity to hurt me." The silence that followed was hollow with despair. "He's the only one I *can* blame."

Ben walked off toward the school.

## Chapter Twelve

It took every ounce of self-control Casey possessed not to peek under the cloth covering Luke's carving. Every day, she sat just a few feet from it, giving Pierrot his reading lesson, tempted to the limit of her self-control to lift an edge of the stained cotton cloth and see the progress Luke had made since the rainstorm that had brought her to the shop for the first time.

Today was no different. As Pierrot closed his book and hurried out the door to make it to the harbor on time, Casey tidied his desk with an eye on the rectangular wooden block she had seen only once. She edged closer, plotting an "accident" that might cause the cloth to fall from the carving. She was standing there beside it pondering her options when the door of the barn opened and the sculptor himself walked in.

He stopped when he saw her and raised an eyebrow.

"Something I can help you with?" he asked.

"Just tidying up," she lied, brushing a wood shaving from the table as if that had been her intention all along.

"You lie like a nun," he said.

She laughed and held up her hands in surrender. "Alright, alright! I won't think about it ever again. Just don't call me a nun!"

The laugh lines at the corner of his eyes deepened as he smiled. He stepped into the shop and closed the door behind him. "The word 'nun' isn't usually the first one that comes to mind when I see you," he admitted with a smirk.

Casey laughed again, moving back to the desk to finish

tidying up. "I'm flattered."

Luke moved closer and leaned back against a dresser that was still under construction. "You really ought to laugh more often," he said.

Casey's cheer froze instantly, struck down by unexpected guilt. She was suddenly reminded of the depth of her sorrow, and these days of greater levity only exacerbated her remorse. She had no right to smile. She certainly had no right to laugh. Though she may not have directly caused the events of that late-August night, she had done nothing to stop them either. In moments like these, the only emotion as intense as her grief was her guilt. She looked around at the half-finished furniture that had seemed warm and comforting moments before. Now, she felt as if it were closing in on her. For the first time in weeks, memories and emotions broadsided her and she found herself fighting both the pain and the frustration of still being their victim.

Luke was taken aback by the sudden transformation in her countenance. "What was that?" he asked.

She shook her head and forced a smile, moving to Pierrot's desk to focus her attention on the sample writing he had done for her that afternoon. She was reaching for a stray piece of paper when Luke pushed off the dresser and stilled her hand by placing one of his on top of it.

"What was that?" he said again, gazing intently at her downcast face. "No," he said when she began to shake her head again, "I'd really like to know." There was no impatience in his voice, no pressure in his words.

"I can't talk about it," she said, a tense edge creeping into her voice as memories hurled themselves against the barriers in her mind.

"If I offended you—" Luke began.

Casey stopped him with a look that begged him to drop the subject.

He considered her fragile, wounded expression, his gaze

narrowing as he began to put the pieces together in his mind. "Is this about what happened before you came?" he asked, referring to the conversation they'd had during her second visit to *Le Bigorneau.* He saw fear and remorse flash across her face. "Of course it is," he said softly.

The heat coming from the stove felt stifling to Casey. When she looked up at Luke, it was with haunted, brave eyes. "It'll pass," she said. Though her present circumstances seemed to contradict the fact, she knew that she had had better days recently, brighter days, and that those offered her tenuous hope.

She turned to stow Pierrot's papers in the desk drawer. "Did you come out here to work on your sculpture?" she asked, attempting to divert Luke's attention from herself.

"Actually, I came out to see if you were here," he answered, causing her to stop in mid-motion.

"Oh," she said.

He smiled. "I was going to see if you wanted to go to an art show opening in Roscoff tonight…"

She was shaking her head before he had finished his explanation.

"But I've got a better idea," he finished.

Before Casey could ask any questions, Luke moved to the stove, opened it, and added a couple logs to the embers still glowing inside. When he'd finished stoking the fire and shut down the air vents to ensure that the logs wouldn't burn too fast, he took Casey's coat from the back of the chair where she had hung it earlier and helped her into it. Too unsettled to argue, she meekly complied, then led the way out of the shop while he held the door for her. They passed through the restaurant, giving Marguerite a wide berth, and stepped out into the moist fog that had become so comforting to Casey.

When she turned instinctively toward home, Luke's hand on her waist guided her in the opposite direction, away from the jetty, the church, and the semaphore. They walked down a narrow street and veered off onto a dirt path when the road turned inland. The path curved with the shoreline, bordered on one side by rock formations plunging down to the water's edge and on the other by vast, flat fields. When they had moved beyond the streetlights, Luke took the lead, offering his hand when the terrain was uneven. Casey breathed in the ripe smell of ocean spray and muddy fields and reveled in the sound of waves breaking against rugged shores. She felt the tension and awkwardness seeping from her as they walked. Her face and hair were damp, but she didn't care. There was something about the deepening darkness, the ocean, and their silent progress that was at once comforting and exhilarating.

"Where are we going?" Casey asked when they had walked for a few minutes.

He didn't answer.

"Is it something I said back there?" There was an embarrassed smile in her voice as she tried to discern what had prompted such a spontaneous evening trek.

"You needed out of there," he said simply.

That much was true, Casey conceded. Though she hadn't realized it at the time, this was exactly what her body and mind had needed to rid her of the memory-induced guilt that had gripped her.

When they came to the foot of the island's lighthouse, Luke took a small path that led to a rounded wooden gate. Just beyond the gate was a small thatch-roof cottage that stood on the edge of a cliff. The rotating beam from the lighthouse glanced over the cottage, revealing pristine white walls, sky blue shutters, and an inset blue door. Luke pulled a bundle of keys from his pocket and waited for the next passage of the lighthouse beam to select the right key and insert it into the lock. Though there were myriad questions going through Casey's mind, she said nothing as Luke reached inside the door and flipped a switch. The front door of the cottage led directly into a large area that was at once a living room and a dining room. To the left, two armchairs and a couch faced a wide fireplace. On the other side of the room, a beautiful table which Casey recognized as Luke's handiwork was framed by six matching chairs. The dining room led into a kitchen whose windows faced the sea. It was a welcoming space, as comfortable as it was beautiful. Casey walked through the room to the wall of windows that gave onto the seascape beyond. Though darkness had fallen, she could hear the waves and catch the occasional reflection of the moon in the water. Luke opened the central glass doors and a gust of ocean air rushed into the room.

There was a wooden deck just outside the doors, enclosed on two ends to break the wind. Luke unfolded two comfortable deck chairs that rested against the outside wall and set them close to the railing at the front of the deck. Casey sat in the chair on the right, a little bemused, while Luke disappeared inside the house and came back with a lit storm lantern and two thick blankets in his hands. He placed the lantern on the far side of the railing, handed a blanket to Casey, and installed himself in the chair next to hers.

Their silence was neither tense nor awkward. It was a shared complicity.

"Warm enough?" Luke asked after several minutes had passed.

Casey, who had snuggled down into her chair and propped her feet on the railing, turned her head against the backrest and nodded sleepily. Though the air was cold and damp, she felt cozy and warm.

"I own two homes on the island," Luke said, answering a question she hadn't asked. "I rent this one out in the summer."

"It's beautiful."

"It's a bit too remote for some tourists."

"I love it," she said sincerely.

A companionable silence settled again. As it stretched, Casey began to wonder if Luke had expected the change of venue to spur her on to revelations she might not have made in the familiar environment of the shop.

She cleared her throat and searched for the right words. "Am I supposed to pour out my guts now?" she asked with a smile, hoping his answer would be in the negative.

She heard the release of air as he chuckled and imagined his laugh lines adding depth to his smile. When she looked over at him, she found his eyes closed and a smile on his lips. He opened one eye and caught her staring. Casey quickly looked away, surprise and embarrassment making her blush.

This time his chuckle was audible. "No gut-spilling necessary," he said. "We can sit in silence if that's what you want."

Casey knew his statement was genuine. One of the many facets of Luke that drew her to him was his ability to sit in utter silence and show neither discomfort nor impatience. It lent him a mystery that seemed suited to this wild land he had adopted. As much as she tried, Casey couldn't imagine him in a place like Paris or encased in the suburban cocoon of Glen Ellyn.

"Tell me about your growing up years," she said softly, knowing he would simply refuse if he didn't feel inclined to speak.

"What do you want to know?"

They were both facing the invisible ocean, eyes closed.

"Do I have a limited number of questions?" she asked with a smile.

"I'll let you know when you've exceeded it," he said.

"You said your parents were missionaries. What did they do?"

Casey hadn't known how to react when Luke had first told her about his parents' profession. His revelation had astounded and shaken her, and though their conversation had lasted a few minutes longer, her heart hadn't been in it. Her first encounter with missionaries had sent her running halfway around the world. What were the odds that she would find the product of another missionary family on a remote island in France? It had taken this long—and the darkness of this place—for her to find the courage to voice her questions.

"They started a church. Spent thirty years of their lives pouring themselves into it."

"Was it large?"

"In attendance?"

She nodded in the lantern light, and though his eyes were closed, he must have heard the movement.

"It fluctuated. Maybe three couples when it began. Just under a hundred by the time they left."

"Not much to show for thirty years," Casey said.

"Not if you evaluate success by numbers," he said.

Casey pondered his statement for a moment and watched the lantern light play over his features before asking her next question.

"Was it hard?"

"Having missionaries for parents?"

She nodded.

"It had its challenges," he conceded.

She waited for him to go on.

"It wasn't popular to be an American in France. And I didn't know how to make myself fit in in the States. I was an enigma in both places. Or an anomaly."

Casey couldn't imagine a young Luke struggling with feelings of alienation. He seemed the kind of man who would be comfortable anywhere.

"Add to that being part of a high profile Christian family," he continued, "and the expectations on both sides of the ocean became completely unattainable."

"They wanted you to be perfect," Casey said.

Luke nodded. "And if we weren't, it was a spiritual flaw." He rose to adjust the wick in the lantern, casting a dimmer light on the patio. "Other people have plain old flaws, missionaries have spiritual flaws," he said, returning to his chair. "It comes with the territory. If you fail, it tarnishes God's image."

"And yet you still believe in divine intervention," Casey said quietly, remembering the statement he had made about his arrival on the island.

"I believe in God," he corrected her.

She tried to read a trace of insincerity in his face but found none. His gaze was steady and unwavering.

"Did you ever wish things were different?"

Luke smiled. "That's an understatement."

"Were your parents happy?"

"They were burned out. Happiness wasn't much of a priority."

"Were *you* happy?"

He pursed his lips in thought and shook his head. "Not really." He turned his head to look at Casey. "I was poor, considered weird most places I went, neglected by parents who worked too hard, and everyone expected me to be perfect."

Casey marveled at his smile. "Great way for God to reward His workers," she murmured.

"I just became a loner," Luke continued without prompting. "It's safer and easier if you don't need anything or anybody."

"Even at boarding school?"

"That was different."

Casey waited for him to say more, but he was silent.

"Were you a loner there?" she prompted.

Another long silence preceded his answer. "Not really. I think I would have loved it if I hadn't been forced to go there."

"By your parents?"

He nodded.

"And you didn't want to go?"

"No. But I made good friends there. Got into a lot of trouble." He smirked at the memories. "Felt like I belonged for the first time in my life." He sighed. "They were probably some of my happiest years, but I didn't want to be there, so I never admitted it."

"So you don't think your parents did the right thing."

He shook his head. "No matter how good the silver linings are, abandoning your child in a strange place against his wishes and blaming it on God is an irreparable mistake."

Casey had a vivid memory of Ben's tormented gaze. "How could they send you away?"

Another silence. "They thought it was the best thing for me. And it *was* for the kids who were there because they wanted to be and had begged their parents to attend the school. They loved being there and they loved seeing their parents during breaks."

"Because they weren't there against their will."

He nodded. "I'm pretty sure their families thrived despite the distance. It was a good thing for them." He paused. "Just not for me."

"Did your parents ever ask you what you thought?"

Casey's voice was sharper and Luke heard the change. He looked at her through hooded eyes. "My parents were far from perfect," he simply stated.

"But they were missionaries!" Casey said with more fervor than she had intended. "They were Christians—they're supposed to care for their children!"

"They cared."

Casey was desperate for Luke to say more but he seemed to have nothing more to add. She was surprised at the bitterness in her own voice when she said, almost to herself, "How can they claim to love God and not love their children?"

"They did love God. They still do. And they loved me. But they thought at the time that He wanted them to send me to boarding school."

"Why would a good God want a child sent away against his wishes?"

"A good God wouldn't."

Casey stared at him for a long time before asking, "So God isn't good?"

Luke sat forward in his seat and looked directly at Casey. "God is good."

Casey's eyes opened wide with disbelief. "How can you believe that when your parents' choice to follow Him cost you so much?"

Luke stared silently for a few moments. "I had to stop believing in man's goodness in order to start believing in God's," he said.

Casey shook her head uncomprehendingly and, exasperated, rose and stepped to the railing, her blanket held around her with one hand.

When Luke spoke again, it was from right behind her. "It's hard to stop blaming God until you can start blaming man."

"But your parents did what they did because God told them to!"

She gripped the railing with a white-knuckled hand and looked up at Luke as he stepped up beside her. Luke reached out and placed his hand over hers, wrapping his warmth around her chilled fingers, stilling her anger with his touch. "They *thought* He'd told them to," he said. "They made an honest mistake for all the right reasons."

Casey shook her head. "It could have destroyed you!"

"It nearly did," he said calmly, staring out into the darkness. "But unless I can learn to forgive their honest mistakes, I'll never be able to forgive my own." he added.

Ben's words filled Casey's memory as she looked out over the water. "I have a former student who would tell you that the reason people make mistakes is because God created them with the ability to do so." She looked beseechingly into his eyes. "He created us to fail. He made us capable of harming others. How could He do that to us? How could He do that to *Ben*?"

Luke turned his unwavering gaze on Casey. His fingers wrapped more tightly around hers, but he didn't ask about this student she had never mentioned before. "God didn't do it to Ben," was all he said.

Hearing Ben's name on Luke's lips startled her. She realized this was the first time she had mentioned him in conversation since August. Her eyes widened with remembered grief.

Luke released Casey's hand and turned to prop himself against the railing, gentleness and compassion softening his features.

"I just don't understand," Casey said, fighting back the tears Luke's touch and Ben's memory had evoked.

He nodded. "I don't either," he said. "But I've spent the last thirteen years getting a clearer picture of who God is—not what flawed humans tell me He is. And what I know of Him tells me it wasn't His intent for me to be neglected—nor His doing." He smiled softly as Casey nodded. "He loves us too much to inflict that kind of pain on us. We bring it on ourselves by the decisions we make. And the consequences sometimes destroy those we love."

Casey took a deep, fragile breath and allowed herself to edge a little closer to Luke's warmth.

"Mind if I smoke?" he asked.

Casey pulled back in surprise. "I had forgotten you smoked."

He raised an eyebrow.

"That first night, when you carried my suitcases, all I could see of you in the dark was the tip of your cigarette." She smiled at the memory, astounded that she was standing in an empty home on this night with the stranger who had rescued her several weeks before.

"Nasty habit I picked up with my no-good Parisian friends." His smile was ironic.

"Do you smoke often?" she asked, realizing he hadn't smoked in her presence yet.

"Rarely," he said. "Usually after a tough day of fishing. Or when I'm really cold."

Casey smiled. "Are you cold now?"

He shook his head. "No." He gave her a half-smile and pulled a pack from his pocket. "Want one?" he offered.

Casey laughed. "Uh, no. Thank you, though."

There was a smile in Luke's eyes as he cupped his hands around the lighter.

## Chapter Thirteen

It was an hour past the time when Pierrot usually started his reading lesson, but the boy still hadn't arrived. Casey had spent the time reading one of the books Pierrot had borrowed from someone on the island, but his lateness was beginning to worry her. He had never missed their appointment before and she wondered what it was that could keep her enthusiastic student from appearing as he had every day for several weeks.

Leaving the shop for a moment, she entered the restaurant and found Luke sitting at one of the tables reading the paper.

"Have you seen Pierrot?" she asked.

Luke looked up at her, then glanced at his watch. "He should have been here over an hour ago," he said.

"Exactly. I'm starting to get worried."

"Let me call his grandfather," he said, getting up and moving toward the phone at the bar. He dialed. "Joseph?" he asked a few moments later.

He listened intently and glanced at Casey.

"Is it Joseph?" he asked.

Casey saw him turn a shade paler as he listened to the reply. He was moving before he put down the receiver. He grabbed two jackets from the coat rack inside the door and handed one to Casey.

"Come on," he said, his features set, his body tense. He led her hastily from the restaurant and set off at a fast pace toward the west side of the island.

"What is it?" Casey asked, struggling to keep up with his strides as a feeling of dread coursed through her body.

"Doctor Duchêne answered the phone. Something's happened to Pierrot."

They arrived at Pierrot's home and entered without knocking.

"*Salut, Luke,*" the doctor said briskly as they entered the living room where Pierrot lay on a stretcher and an elderly man, presumably his grandfather, sat on a worn couch flanked by two men. He tried to rise, but one of the men pulled him back down, ordering him curtly to stay put until the police arrived. The grandfather mumbled something unintelligible and stared at his grandson through alcohol-glazed eyes. There were two women standing at Pierrot's side with the doctor. He held a thick stack of gauze against Pierrot's chest where his bloody shirt had been cut away.

Casey felt her blood turn cold. She halted in the doorway and her heart began to pound loudly in her ears. Luke strode immediately to Pierrot's side, conferring quietly with the doctor and laying a hand on the boy's arm in a paternal way. When Pierrot turned his head toward Luke, Casey felt an overwhelming surge of relief. He was alive.

Luke gently instructed the young man to save his strength and glanced at Casey. All it took was one look at her stricken face to bring him to her side. "The doctor says he'll probably be alright," he said, a hand on her arm, his voice calm and his words precise. "We just need to get him to Roscoff as soon as possible."

Casey looked past him at the pale boy lying on the stretcher. "What happened?" she asked voicelessly, her lungs incapable of supplying the breath necessary for sound.

"From what his neighbors gather," he said, glancing toward the men sitting on the couch with Pierrot's grandfather, "it was accidental. He was drunk and cleaning his rifle…"

"Pierrot was shot?" The horror of it made Casey sway.

Luke gripped her shoulders to steady her as he nodded. "You need to sit down?"

She shook her head, taking in the grey color of Pierrot's skin and the occasional low moans coming from his white lips. "What are they waiting for?" she asked. "Shouldn't they be getting him to a hospital?"

"They'll move him as soon as the call comes from the port. They're waiting for the ferry to get here."

Casey felt her breath coming in shorter gasps as panic began to petrify her thinking. Luke felt her sway again and locked his gaze with hers. "Breathe deeply, Casey," he said, shaking her a little when she didn't respond. "Casey." His voice was firm and drew her mind back to the present from the morbid past. Her eyes darted to Pierrot, then back to Luke. She shook her head and took a step backward.

"I can't stay here," she said, trying to back into the entrance hall.

Luke's grip on her arms tightened and kept her immobile.

"He needs you here," he said.

She shook her head again, threatening hysteria sharpening her voice. "No, he doesn't," she said, raising a hand to her throat in horror. "I…" Her thoughts were sluggish. "I just can't stay here."

Luke gave her another searching look before releasing her and moving to Pierrot's side.

"Casey is here," she heard him whisper in French.

Pierrot's lips moved, but no words came out.

"Would you like to see her?" Luke asked softly.

Pierrot gave an imperceptible nod. Luke looked up and met Casey's gaze. He didn't say a word. There was neither a challenge nor a command in his eyes. He simply waited, his hand on Pierrot's bare forearm.

Casey held his gaze and willed herself to step forward. Her limbs were unbearably heavy. Her balance less than steady.

Panic rose in her like bile, but she fought it down and, with Luke's gaze lending her courage, took several more steps until she stood next to her student.

Luke took her hand and placed it where his had been on Pierrot's arm. She looked down to where her fingers felt the cold, dry surface of Pierrot's skin. Her eyes ran up his arm to the bloody gauze on his shoulder. She felt panic again rising to the surface and was about to snatch her hand back when Pierrot's feeble voice broke the silence.

"Casey," he said on a feeble breath.

Her eyes snapped to his face and found his eyes half-open and turned toward her. With no further thought for the turmoil in her mind, she moved so he could see her better and attempted a shaky smile.

"Hi," she said, and when her voice failed to work, said it again. She mustered a more confident smile and lifted her free hand to brush a strand of hair off his feverish forehead. "You're going to be alright," she said quietly, feeling Luke's presence behind her like a wall of courage.

Pierrot nodded feebly. Casey was conscious of a phone ringing somewhere in the house and of one of the neighbor ladies heading out to answer it. The doctor stood across from Casey, keeping pressure on the young man's wound and monitoring his vital signs. She kept her eyes on Pierrot's face and stroked his arm, afraid to break the contact in any way.

A hand on her shoulder startled her. She turned her head and heard Luke say, "The ferry's on its way. We need to move him."

Casey nodded and stepped back. One of the men rose off the couch, replaced immediately by the largest of the two women who had been standing by the stretcher. The other woman entered from the hallway with a heavy blanket and draped it over Pierrot's inert form. With the islander at the front of the stretcher and Luke at the back, they maneuvered the young man out of the living room, down the hall, and into the street where a tractor waited. They loaded the boy onto the trailer at the back of the tractor and the doctor climbed on next to him. Luke held a hand out to Casey to help her up. She didn't move, unsure that she had the courage to face whatever lay ahead. He stepped toward her and led her to the trailer's edge, assisting her onto it with a gentle hand.

They made the drive to the *embarcadère* in silence, and Casey worried with every bump in the uneven road that the jostling would worsen Pierrot's condition. Two uniformed police officers disembarked as soon as the ferry docked, then, with the help of the captain, they loaded the stretcher onto the boat. The ferry immediately set off toward Roscoff. Casey resumed her position at Pierrot's side, her eyes on his face, following the doctor's instructions to keep pressure on the dressing while he continued to monitor his patient's pulse and blood pressure. Luke conferred briefly with the captain, the same man who had piloted the boat that had brought Casey to the island months ago. She was surprised to see the weathered, stoic man give Luke a friendly pat as he left the wheelhouse and moved aft toward Casey. He stopped next to her, his features drawn, his breathing heavy. He rested one hand on the blankets covering his young friend's leg and occasionally asked succinct questions of Doctor Duchêne. Casey didn't dare look away from the young man who was now shaking under her touch, but the sense of Luke's presence near her reassured and quieted her.

When they had reached Roscoff and loaded Pierrot's stretcher into the waiting ambulance, Luke led Casey quickly across the street to a car parked in a distant lot. He took a set of keys from his pocket and unlocked Casey's door before installing himself in the car and turning the key in the ignition. They set off in the same direction the ambulance had gone.

It was close to midnight when Luke parked the car near the Roscoff pier and turned off the ignition. They sat in silence for a moment, reliving the day's drama. Pierrot had had surgery to repair the damage done by his grandfather's rifle, and the bullet had miraculously done no irreparable harm. When they had last seen him, he'd been sedated and bandaged, but some of the color had returned to his cheeks and lips. They had stood silently at his bedside, each wrestling with their own emotions, then had headed back to the island for the night.

Casey let her head fall back against the headrest and closed her eyes. The silence and immobility numbed her. She couldn't remember the last time she had been conscious of anything outside the image of Pierrot's face alternating with Ben's in her mind. Every time she had smiled into his beseeching eyes, she had been smiling at Ben. Every time she had told him he would be okay, she had been speaking to Ben. Every time she had willed away tears of helplessness and frustration, she had been grieving for Ben.

Ben was so present in her mind that she briefly imagined it was he who shifted in the seat next to hers. When she opened her eyes, it was Luke she saw. He leaned forward, his forehead resting against his arms crossed on the steering wheel, and breathed heavily. The slant of his shoulders reflected utter exhaustion, and Casey knew it went far beyond the physical. Casey longed to comfort him but didn't know how. After a few moments, he sat back and stared ahead, weariness altering the features of his face and making him look suddenly years older.

His lassitude reflected her own. Her eyes felt swollen though she hadn't shed a tear. Her neck and shoulders seemed immobilized by tension. She rotated her head from side to side and tried to relieve the strain.

"You did well," Luke said without turning to look at her.

She smiled sadly and shook her head. Luke looked at her then. "You did well," he repeated.

Casey's eyes locked on his. "I would have run if you hadn't made me stay."

He held her gaze for long moments, weighing his words against the memories he saw in her eyes. Casey looked away. They were at the very edge of the parking lot, where the ground gave way to the ocean that extended into the darkness that was the Ile de Batz. She was searching the horizon for traces of light when Luke spoke again.

"Tell me about Ben."

And Casey felt her stomach heave with the realization that she couldn't refuse to answer his plea. This had been Ben's day as much as it had been Pierrot's, and his memory permeated every fragment of the reality that froze her to the bone like the cold ocean air buffeting the car and blowing through her very core. It took no effort for Casey to travel back to the August night that had disemboweled her life. Memories washed over her and drowned her in raw, shrieking waves.

The ringing phone brought Casey out of a sound sleep. She reached toward the sound and felt blindly along her nightstand for the cordless receiver she had placed within reach. The phone was about to ring for the fourth time, forwarding the call to her answering machine, when her fingers closed around the receiver.

"Hello?" Her voice was hoarse from sleep. She squinted at the alarm clock next to her bed. Four twenty-three. Casey was suddenly alert. No good news came in the middle of the night.

"Miss Jensen." Ben's voice was ragged.

"Ben?"

"Yep," he said, his tone a little off.

"Ben, where are you?"

"I'm in town." His words sounded slurred.

Casey tried to sound casual. "What are you doing in town at this time of night, Ben?"

"Oh… Little bit of this, little bit of that."

"Have you been drinking, Ben?" He didn't sound coherent.

"No, Miss Jensen," he said too earnestly, "I'm just high on life." He laughed giddily. "I've got the joy of Jesus in my heart!" he exclaimed hysterically, letting out an uncharacteristic whoop. From the crackling in the connection, Casey could tell he was on a cell-phone.

"Ben, tell me where you are."

His voice bellowed an off-pitch version of the old Led Zeppelin classic. "And I'm buying a stairway to heaven…"

"Ben, can you pay attention please? I need to know where you are."

He wasn't listening to her. "So I had this little conversation with god earlier tonight," he said, pausing to take a long breath between sentences. "And here's what the big guy told me: if I really want to find out if he's out there, I've got to take the first step."

His voice was fading in and out, and Casey suspected that he was gesticulating wildly as he spoke.

"What kind of a step are you talking about Ben?" She was pulling clothes and shoes on, not sure what she would do once she was dressed, but feeling the desperate need to be ready to rush out and rescue her troubled student.

"No, god. *God*'s talking about the step."

"What kind of step is God talking about?"

There was a pause. "A reeeeeally big one," Ben said in an eerily cheerful voice.

"Ben, where are you?" Casey repeated.

"I'm hitchin' a ride to god."

"Where is God, Ben."

"Silly girl," she heard him say. He giggled a little before adding, "God's in Heaven. He's waaaayyyy up in heaven where people like me can't crap on his parade."

"Ben…"

"Actually, he's probably on the phone to my parents right now, saying 'Yo, Landons, do something about your kid before he ruins my reputation.'"

"Tell me how you're getting to heaven, Ben." Casey was rushing around the living room looking for her purse.

"Miss Jensen, you're a reeeeeally cool person."

"Ben! Listen to me!" She located her purse and fumbled for her cell phone.

"And I want you to know that you did your best. Seriously. I mean, everybody else would have told me to get lost but you just kept on reading my crap and looking all concerned and stuff."

"You're a very good writer, Ben," she said into her phone while she dialed 9-1-1 on her cell.

"Have you been writing tonight?" She covered the mouthpiece when the 9-1-1 operator picked up.

Casey spoke fast, afraid to go too long without speaking to Ben. She gave her name and address and explained the situation as briefly as possible. "I have one of my students on the other line. His name is Ben Landon. His family lives on Beverly. He sounds intoxicated and keeps talking like he's going to commit suicide. Is there anything you can do?"

She switched back to Ben. "Ben, tell me where you are. Please."

The operator was speaking into her other ear. "Can you try to find out his location, ma'am?"

"Are you in Glen Ellyn, Ben?"

He was beginning to sound angry. "I *told* you I'm going on a little trip. God and me are going to have a beer and discuss who screwed up my life—him or me."

"Miss Jensen," came the operator's voice, "ask him what he can see from where he is."

"Ben, can you look around and tell me what you see?"

He was singing "Jesus Loves Me" at the top of his lungs.

"Ben!"

"'Little ones to him belong...'"

"What can you see from where you are, Ben? Do you see street signs or buildings?"

"I see angels," he said. "Lots and lots of angels with all their halos lined up in a row."

"I need to know where you are, Ben," Casey's voice was hoarse. She could hear the operator talking to patrol cars, but felt powerless to give them any precise information. Her chest ached. She couldn't breathe past the sobs lodged in her throat. She thought of landmarks he might recognize.

"Do you see the movie theater, Ben?"

"Nope. No more movies for Ben," he said pleasantly. "Hey, could you tell my parents something for me?"

"No, Ben, you can tell them yourself."

"Now you're being silly again," he said in a voice he might have used to address his little sister.

"Ben, can you see the high school? Are you near home?"

"Home?" He laughed in a way that made Casey's blood run cold.

"What else can I do?" Casey begged the emergency operator. She started to sob.

"Keep him on the phone, ma'am. Try to stay calm so he doesn't get excited."

Ben was singing again. He stopped abruptly and said, "So here's the message for my parents. Are you there?"

"Yes, Ben. I'm right here." She covered her face with her hand and desperately strove for composure.

"Tell them that they should have been more like you."

Casey sank to the floor, no longer able to stand.

"'cause you're a really cool person," he said again. Then quickly, "Hey, there's my ride!"

Casey pressed the receiver to her ear. "Ben!" she pleaded, "Tell me where you are!"

And then she heard a sound that knocked the breath from her lungs. She fumbled with her cell phone and dropped it twice before getting it to her ear. "I can hear a train!" she shrieked at the emergency operator. "I can hear a train!" she sobbed. "I think he's on the tracks. Go help him! Please. *Please* go help him!" She spoke anxiously into the other receiver. "Ben?"

*"Jesus loves me this I know…"*

"Ben, listen to me!!"

*"For the Bible tells me so…"*

"Please don't do this, Ben. Please, Ben. *Ben!!*"

*"Little ones to Him…"*

There was the horrifying shriek of brakes, the repeated blast of a horn, the clatter of a cell phone falling and bouncing.

Then nothing.

Casey heard a long, raucous shriek—hoarse, broken, and guttural. It went on for an eternity and ended in agonizing, ragged sobs.

She never realized it was coming from her.

∞

Casey didn't know how long they'd been sitting there. The wind still howled and the waves still crashed invisibly against the shore.

Her body felt as if it had been crushed by a giant hand and hurled into the car seat with shattering force. She sat in stunned silence, hunched over her crossed arms, staring with wide, horror-filled eyes at the dashboard of Luke's car. Luke sat near, his hand moving slowly across her back. He was real. And he was solid. She heard the sound of her breath being drawn painfully through her constricted throat.

She couldn't remember the words she had used to tell Ben's story. She only knew that visual markers had surfaced in her mind and remembered conversations had stolen from her lips as she had opened the floodgates of her memory. Ben's first talk with her after her comments on *The Little Prince*. His letters and poems. The rumors. Her encounter with the Landons and their son's disappearance from school. At some point in her recitation, the story had begun to tell itself, and she'd become aware only of the emotions attached to each recollection. They had swirled into a vortex that had spun her from the present into the unbearable past and left her huddled on the passenger seat of an immobile car in the middle of the night.

Luke's hand stroked warmth against her back. She willed herself to take deeper, steadying breaths.

"You couldn't have saved him," Luke said quietly.

She shook her head. "You don't know that." Her words settled in the lengthening silence.

Luke expelled a deep breath and dropped his head back against his headrest. "Except that I once stood in his shoes."

Casey said nothing. She wasn't sure she wanted her guilt assuaged. She slowly sat back, instantly missing the comfort of his hand, but needing to see the honesty of his eyes.

Luke turned his head toward her and met her gaze. "I didn't choose train tracks," he said quietly, "but my goal was the same. I climbed to the top of a crane in a construction site near my school and told myself to step off."

A shiver of horror shook Casey.

"I'd decided to confront God myself, since no one else seemed to have any answers."

"What happened?" Her voice was soft and hoarse.

"I made the decision not to jump," he said. "Which only confirmed how much of a coward I was."

Casey stared mutely.

Luke shifted in his seat to face Casey. "And Ben made his decision," he continued. "You loved him. You helped him. You wanted the best for him. But *Ben* made his decision. And it was nothing you could *un*make for him."

"I should have warned his parents."

"You did."

"I should have tried to talk him out of it." Her eyes clung earnestly to his.

"You did."

"I should have been there."

"He didn't want you there."

"I should have said something to convince him…"

"He didn't want convincing."

"But he was just the *victim*!" Casey persisted, her anger mounting along with heart-crushing sorrow. "He didn't ask for *any* of it!"

Luke reached across the space between them and gently turned her face toward him, anchoring her gaze to his. "You did all you could do."

She shook off his hand, her voice cracking with the vehemence of her denial. "I should have…"

He repeated, more forcefully, "You did all you could do."

"*Then why did he do it??*" It was a cry that had been months in the making and it tore the dam from Casey's pain, releasing a tidal wave of gut-wrenching powerlessness.

"Why did he kill himself?" she begged brokenly, harsh sobs convulsing her body and sending her staggering from the car as she vomited the horror of her despair onto the gravel of the deserted parking lot.

Luke was instantly at her side, kneeling with her, anchoring her to his warmth, draping her with his courage. His cheek rested against her hair when her retching eased. The world seemed to tilt and she leaned more heavily against the strength that emanated from his presence.

"You did nothing wrong," he whispered roughly, his mouth just above her ear. "Ben's parents made their decisions. *They* neglected him. *They* forced him into a life he couldn't tolerate. *They* ignored your warnings—and probably God's. And then *Ben* decided to take his life in spite of the love and support you gave him. Not because your friendship wasn't enough, but because his pain was too great. *He* decided. And there's nothing you could have done to alter that."

Casey looked blindly out across the water and whispered, "But why did he call me then?"

She felt Luke's arm tighten around her. "Because you loved him."

## Chapter Fourteen

Several minutes later, Luke and Casey boarded the ferry. Casey knew it was well past regular hours and was grateful that the captain had waited for them before heading back to the Ile de Batz for the night. Luke shook his hand and thanked him as he boarded the boat, reaching back to assist Casey. The captain asked about Pierrot and Luke filled him in on the details.

As the boat left the *embarcadère*, Casey settled onto a cold plastic bench in the enclosed cabin. Luke joined her a few moments later.

"Will you go to the hospital with me tomorrow?" he asked.

She nodded, exhausted. "I didn't know you owned a car."

He smiled. "It's an old beater, but it serves its purpose."

"You really think Pierrot's going to be alright?" she asked.

"I trust his doctors."

"What's going to happen to his grandfather?"

Luke shrugged. "We'll find out in the morning. If he doesn't serve time, he'll at least be put in a home off the island. Either way, Pierrot won't be forced to live with him again."

Casey considered the boy's future. She couldn't imagine him in a foster home, yet she doubted he had any relatives who would take him in.

The blast of the ferry's horn made Casey jump. Luke chuckled at her and shifted in his seat, stretching out his legs and leaning back against the plastic backrest.

"Why does he *do* that?" Casey asked in exasperation,

remembering that the same apparently random blast had startled her on her first trip to the island as well.

Luke chuckled again and slid down farther in his uncomfortable seat to rest his head on top of the backrest. "It's Roland's personal tradition," he explained. "He sounds the horn every time he rounds this end of the island."

Casey contemplated the uncomfortable position Luke had assumed and decided to give it a try. She slid down in her chair until her legs were stretched out in front of her and her head rested at an awkward angle against the backrest. "What for?" she asked.

Luke swiveled his head toward her. "His wife is buried over there," he said, nodding toward the part of the island that held a small cemetery. "It's his way of honoring her, I guess."

Casey thought of the captain's weathered features and hard eyes. "He doesn't seem the type to be sentimental," she said.

"They weren't a conventional couple, but they were devoted. She died three years ago from cancer."

It was a side of the gruff man she wouldn't have suspected. "How do people ever go on with life after something like that?" she wondered out loud, exhaustion in her voice.

She felt Luke's eyes on her. "The same way he does," he said. "He gives kids like Pierrot a job he doesn't deserve. He waits around to get people like us back to the island in the middle of the night. Every good thing he does for someone else honors his wife's memory."

Casey closed her eyes and took a deep breath.

"Just like your kindness to Pierrot honors Ben's," Luke finished.

She smiled wearily.

∞

Casey crawled off the couch the third time the doorbell rang. She fought back another wave of nausea and leaned against the edge of the buffet until it passed. Her legs felt leaden and the walk from the couch to the door left her breathless. The sun coming through the glass on either side of her front door assaulted her senses. She leaned her forehead against the cool wood and shut her eyes against the glare.

"Go away, Layle," she begged through the door. Her body was heavy, saturated with grief and parasited by pain, every cell a raw nerve ending.

"It's Janet Landon, Miss Jensen."

Casey's knees gave out and she clutched the doorknob for support. Grief engulfed her again, submerged her, invaded her, and tore back out of her. She raised a lifeless hand and somehow managed to unlock her door. She pulled it open just far enough to see Janet Landon standing on her doorstep. She closed her eyes and breathed into the pain.

Janet's voice came from far away. "I wanted to come by," she said.

Casey opened her eyes and stared.

"To thank you."

Casey looked away. She would accept condemnation and hatred. She could not tolerate gratitude.

"I had hoped to see you at the funeral, but since you weren't there…"

Casey's mind followed a familiar, horrifying path to visions of Ben in a satin cushioned coffin. Ben without a face. Ben without limbs. Ben shattered, bleeding. Ben giggling shrilly—gruesomely. *"Jesus loves me, this I know…"*

Janet Landon went on. "He left instructions. I don't know if you were aware."

Casey closed her eyes. She breathed in spite of herself.

"He wanted this to come to you."

She shook her head. She wouldn't open her eyes. She wouldn't look.

"There's an envelope at the back," Janet continued in a soft, resolute voice. "It has your name on it. In his handwriting."

She opened her eyes then—and heard her body moan as grief coursed into her and grated over raw, abraded pain.

Janet held out the black notebook.

Casey shook her head. "I can't take that," she tried to say, but only her lips moved.

"He wanted you to have it," Janet said. Then, through tears, added, "We don't deserve to keep it." She bent and placed the notebook on the floor just inside Casey's door. "He trusted you," she said, raising her hand to touch Casey's fingers where they gripped the doorjamb. "He really trusted you," she said again.

Casey closed the door as Janet Landon turned to leave. She slid down the door to the floor and felt a dry heave grip her, then pass. She touched the well-worn black cover. She traced the angry title. Then she lay down on the cold tile of the entryway, her cheek against the notebook. And for the first time in nearly a week, she slept.

They didn't speak as they walked up the hill toward Casey's house. They carried the toll of the day with them, and the intensity of its emotions burdened their progress. Luke pushed open the gate at the bottom of the yard and escorted Casey to the door. She had begun to leave it unlocked, as all the islanders did. It swung open on squeaky hinges and Casey stepped inside to flip the light switch.

Luke stood on the doorstep, his face illuminated by the light streaming through the doorway. There was weariness and strength in his gaze. His hair was disheveled and several days of beard growth darkened his features, but his presence seemed to Casey just as comforting and salutary as it had been her first night on the Ile de Batz. She thought of the convoluted journeys that had led each of them to this place and shook her head in amazement.

"What are the odds that I'd run into the son of American missionaries on the Ile de Batz?" she asked.

He smiled and raised an eyebrow. "Divine providence?"

The miracle of it sent a shiver of awe down her spine. "God," she said with assurance.

Luke smiled, laugh lines creasing his dark skin.

Casey let out a deep breath and leaned against the doorframe. "I tried to hate Him," she said, looking off into the darkness. "After Ben died. I tried to hate Him as much as Ben did."

Luke nodded in understanding, leaning a shoulder against the wall across from Casey.

Casey thought for a moment. "I still don't understand it. I was so sure God was going to save him. And when He didn't…" She looked up at Luke with earnest eyes. "I guess it just made sense to side with Ben. God was either a fabrication or a sadistic tyrant."

"Grief," Luke said simply.

Casey nodded. "And guilt. And this…mind-numbing anger. A God who allowed Ben's misery and suicide didn't deserve my faith."

A long moment passed. Casey let her eyes wander upward toward patches of clear sky and distant stars.

"But you needed Him," Luke said softly.

Casey's eyes filled with tears. "So did Ben."

He nodded in understanding. "The difference is that you choose to trust in His goodness in spite of all that still doesn't make sense."

As Luke said the words, Casey realized how true they were. "I guess I do," she said quietly, sobered by the realization. She wasn't sure when she had come to choose trust over hate or what had lent her the strength to do so. Probably a combination of factors: the passage of time, the rugged beauty of this desolate island, the tale of Luke's journey from anger to serenity, Pierrot's injury and survival and the clarity the release of emotions had allowed. Even the enmity of the islanders who wanted her gone had played a role in bringing her back into Life. The transformation had happened subtly, she realized now, but she stood on the doorstep of her home in the middle of the night a much different woman than she had been mere weeks ago. She knew her recovery was just beginning and that the road ahead would be strewn with emotional and spiritual hurdles, but she had rediscovered God during her exile to the island, and though the mysteries of grief and loss still burdened her, she was prepared to trust blindly in the only One whose comfort made them bearable.

After a comfortable silence, Luke pushed away from the doorframe, his hands still in his pockets, and quietly offered, "I'll be by in the morning."

Casey nodded. "Pierrot's going to be okay, right?" she asked, craving reassurance.

"I think so." He pulled a hand from his pocket and wearily rubbed the back of his neck. "The ten o'clock ferry okay?" he asked.

"I'll be ready by nine thirty."

Luke took a step toward her and kissed her cheek. She heard a soft "Goodnight" whispered close to her ear and instinctively reached up to hug him.

"Thank you," she said, feeling his face against hers as his arms encircled her.

They embraced for a moment longer before he released her. He gave her a long, enigmatic stare before he raised a hand and turned to go.

Casey watched him walk down the path, then turn and head toward *Le Bigorneau*. She closed the door and rested her forehead on its cool surface. A few deep breaths later, she wearily entered the living room, opening the buffet drawer and retrieving Ben's notebook from the darkness. She sank into the leather chair by the fireplace and opened the book's cover. Her fingers trailed down page after page of Ben's weeping heart. As she read, she grieved for him again—and loved him again.

When she reached the envelope at the back of the notebook, her hand hovered indecisively for a moment. She wondered when he had penned his final message and what had prompted him to make his last entry a letter to her. She wanted to read it—she needed to read it—yet she dreaded the words she would find.

With shaking fingers, she tore the envelope open and retrieved the single sheet of paper inside. She felt her chest constrict even before she began to read. Love and sadness conflicted in every cell of her body.

*Dear Miss Jensen,*

*I found this passage while I was sifting through the remains of my French notes and papers. I know you know it well, and yet… I am the fox. If god exists, I thank him for you.*

*"The fox said, 'If you tame me, it will be as if the sun came to shine on my life. I shall know the sound of a step that will be different from all the others. Other steps send me hurrying back underneath the ground. Yours will call me, like music, out of my burrow."*

*Thank you for sitting with me when no one else would. Thank you for understanding me. Thank you for the sound of your footsteps. You have been mercy to me. And love. There are no words to express how grateful I am…*

*Please know that you did nothing wrong—and could have done no more.*

*B.*

Casey went to the window, Ben's letter in her hand. Only the dim glow of fog-shrouded streetlamps bled light into the island's darkness. Dawn would come quickly with its share of challenges, failures, and pain. But it would bring time too. For fuller understanding. For deeper peace. For sweeter joy.

Casey stood by the window until the horizon brightened and the first shutters groaned open in the damp morning silence. Every moment brimmed with healing and whispered hope. A seagull cried. The ferry's horn rang out.

The tide flowed in again.

## *The End*

# A Note from the Author

The plight of missionaries' kids (MKs) is not foreign to me. As the daughter of missionaries to France, I benefited from the best a life in ministry has to offer—and suffered from some of the worst. My work brought me back to Europe where I taught for thirteen years in the boarding school I had attended as a teenager. The students I met there are the inspiration for this story, some of the most memorable of them combined in the character of Benjamin James Landon. My prayers and hopes for them are incarnated in Luke: the survivor who sought until he understood; the victim who identified the human sources of his pain and ceased blaming his Creator for the abandonment, alienation, and suffering in his life; the broken soul who eventually healed and learned to love and *be loved* again.

I in no way intend to imply that all MKs suffer from parental neglect and a consequent anger toward God. Many of them flourish and become leaders of the Christian world, their lives and ministries enriched by their broad horizons and incomparable experiences. Nor do I mean to condemn boarding schools—students who are there of their own volition with frequent, honest communication with their parents thrive. My message is simply that some children of missionaries are the unacknowledged martyrs of our church's endeavor to reach the world for Christ. The Bible is unquestionably clear in the priorities it sets out for believers: God, then family, *then* ministry. If this novel will shed a light on the plight of some of our faith's youngest, most overlooked heroes and inspire missionaries to put their children's welfare first, my goal will have been achieved. Let us never blame God for the pain we cause our children, even inadvertently.

This book is for Riley and Chance, two of the missionary world's most wounded, precious, beautiful souls. Riley, your grave will forever be a testament to missionary zeal gone tragically awry. You shared your Shadowlands with me—they challenge and embolden me still.

Chance, you took a risk by trusting this undeserving teacher and allowing me to know and love you. May your answers be as overwhelming as your doubts—and may serenity and wholeness finally be yours.

*Michèle*

Excerpts from "The Little Prince" used
with permission from Harcourt, Inc.

Cover photo by Mark Rasmussen

For additional pictures, information, and interaction about
"The Edge of Tidal Pools": **www.tidalpoolsonline.com**

Printed in the United States
39681LVS00001B/1-30